About the Author

Len Driscoll is the pen name for author Frank Dirscherl, best known for his many novels in *The Wraith Dread Avenger of the Underworld* series, including the Amazon bestselling *The Wraith* and *Sanderson of Metro,* as well as several short stories. *The Broken Chain* is his first detective novel.

A librarian with over thirty years experience, Frank has also worked at a book wholesaler, a specialist medical practice and as a tutor in the writing and producing of comic books. His interests include reading, traveling, politics, architecture and the environment.

Frank lives in the Illawarra on the south coast of New South Wales, Australia, with his wife and daughter, and is always working on his latest literary endeavors.

GLOWING EYES MEDIA

Praise for *Sanderson of Metro*
Amazon bestseller

"Once shrouded in mystery, The Wraith's stunning origin is finally revealed. Dirscherl and Nash have written one hell of an adventure novel filled with myth, intrigue, and excitement. Highly recommended reading."

> – A.P. Fuchs, writer, *The Axiom-man Saga, The Way of the Fog, Undead World trilogy*

"Recommended for Wraith and pulp hero fans."

> – Leon Mallett, *Amazon*

"At the end of the day, this novel is a worthy addition to The Wraith's continuing story and a necessary purchase if you're a fan of the character. It's also just a flat out enjoyable reading experience."

> – Marcus Bucklin, *Amazon*

"The story is well written, and the Paul Sanderson character fleshed out fairly well...I highly recommend this well written entry for all comic book fans."

> – Virginia E. Johnson, *Amazon*

Praise for *The Wraith*
Amazon bestseller

"I love the coloring job and specially the 'glowing' eyes on the chest of the character."
> – Guillermo del Toro, director, *Blade II, Hellboy I & II*

"I liked the story a lot... It's a very strong debut."
> Steve Englehart, writer, *Detective Comics, The Avengers, Green Lantern*

"I have read the novel (I couldn't put it down)... It is amazing to see how her (Leena) character evolves from Part I to Part II. At first she appears as every other 'girlfriend' in an action film, but those twelve months that pass obviously change her as a person and I love the person she becomes: tougher, but still human."
> – Amber Moelter, actress, *Catwoman: Copycat*

"I finished *The Wraith* book last night. I must say I enjoyed it quite a bit. The scenes kept playing in my head like a big budget Hollywood film. I mentioned earlier that I enjoy when the hero is put to the test physically and doesn't win the battle unscathed. Boy, (Frank) delivered that in spades!"
> – Jeff Welborn, artist, *Nightmare World, The Wraith*

"Genius + sweat + dedication = hard hittin' hero action! Go Aussie!"
> – Dan Lennard, writer, *People* magazine

"*The Wraith* is a wonderful throwback to the purple prose of the bloody pulps with a hero clearly descendant from the likes of the Shadow and the Spider. A fast, action-packed thrill-ride with great characters, both noble and villainous. Slam-bang kick off to a super new series. One I'm anxious to follow."

– Ron Fortier, writer, *The Spider, Brother Bones, Domino Lady*

"I became familiar with Frank Dirscherl's The Wraith from the comic book of the same name. When the first Wraith novel came out I just had to read it. I was not disappointed. The Wraith is a fast-paced thrill-ride. I'm looking forward to the upcoming sequel."

– Bobby Nash, writer, *Evil Ways, Fantastix, Lance Star*

"*The Wraith* (is) a really fun read. Have been a fan of Kenneth Robeson's Doc Savage and The Avenger books for years... *The Wraith* reminds me of Robeson at his best."

– G.R. Lawson, Publisher, General Jinjur Comics

"A short, pulp, superhero novel... Clearly more adventures to come with how this is set up."

– Richard Scott, *Super Reader* website

"*The Wraith* is an enlightening journey into the darkness of superhero fiction, and a worthy entry into both pulpdom and comicdom."

– Kevin Noel Olson, *Silver Bullet Comics* website

Praise for *Valley of Evil*

"The second Wraith novel is an improvement, I think. Right from the start Dirscherl throws you into the middle of crazy action.... This book is a whole lot of superheroic pulp fun, and the good news is there seems to be more to come...I look forward to some more of the same."

> – Richard Scott, *Super Reader* website

"I think (Dirscherl) really captured a noir element with (his) voice."

> – Joshua Gamon, writer, *Abigail & Rox, Digital Webbing Presents*

"I did quite enjoy the books. Best of all, it wasn't overly sex-filled or gory—I can't stand most modern superhero comics that show such things or have the heroes just swear and swear. So *The Wraith* (and *Valley of Evil*) was just up my alley."

> – Greg Gick, writer, *The Werewolf of Rutherford Grange, Tales of the Shadowmen, Secret Agent X Vol. 2*

"The Dread Avenger is back. After battling the Cobra in his first prose adventure, The Wraith returns to face all new challenges from Metro City's greatest villains, most notably Hong Kong drug kingpin Ma Tzi. As with his first Wraith novel, Frank Dirscherl treats us to a pulp-inspired adventure that keeps readers on the edge of their seat. You have to read this novel in one sitting."

> – Bobby Nash, writer, *Evil Ways, Fantastix, Lance Star*

Praise for *Crossfire*

"Stephen did a fantastic job of bringing Frank Dirscherl's character to life!"
- Adam DiTroia, composer, *The Wraith: Eyes of Judgment*, MTV, Fox Sports

"Loved the book!! Can't wait for the next installment..."
- Larry Mainland, actor, *The Walking Dead, Lawless, The Three Stooges*

"The action comes swift, and doesn't stop until the final pages. *Crossfire* tells a great story of betrayal and revenge."
- C.R. Blevins, writer, *A Western Tale*

"This was my first introduction to The Wraith and I was not disappointed. The action comes swift, and doesn't stop until the final pages.... If you love a good action/hero story, you will certainly enjoy reading *Crossfire*."
- Ally, *Amazon*

"Makes me want more...should be the next series on Netflix..."
- Bill Lancaster, *Amazon*

"Another excellent entry in The Wraith Adventures series. Thoroughly recommended for Wraith fans and fans of pulp super-heroics."
- Leon Mallett, *Amazon*

Praise for *Vendetta*

"...in all a great brew that had me hooked for the whole ride. Now bring on the next book, Frank..."

– Leon Mallett, *Amazon*

"This book starts with a literal bang and doesn't let the foot off of the gas until the very last page. The book is well plotted and moves at a breakneck pace, making it an enjoyable, short read. I loved this book very much as a fan of The Wraith and I believe that anyone who is a fan of the series should consider this required reading."

– Marcus Bucklin, *Amazon*

Praise for *Zombies Attack!* in *Metahumans vs the Undead*

"This compilation of superheroes vs evil offers top entertainment for superhero lovers! Frank Dirscherl and others are at their best with their contributed stories. I will now pursue other stories written by these authors, such as those involving Mr. Dirscherl's The Wraith. This type of reading enjoyment knows no end!"

–   Ramona Wingart, writer, *Where is Brother Beaver?,*
Emily Suzanne Smith!

Praise for *Werewolves Attack!* in *Metahumans vs Werewolves*

"Always a great read. Can never put it down once you get started... "

BY FRANK DIRSCHERL

FICTION

the *George 'Magpie' Collins mystery* series (writing as Len Driscoll)

1. *The Broken Chain*
2. *The Black Seam* - COMING SOON
3. *The Magpie's Shadow* - COMING SOON

The Wraith Dread Avenger of the Underworld series

1. *The Wraith*
2. *Valley of Evil*
3. *Crossfire* (with Stephen J. Semones)
4. *Cult of the Damned*
5. *Cry of the Werewolf*
6. *Swamp Witch of Satan's Forest* (with Ray MacKay)
7. *Vendetta*
8. *Lady Wraith* (with Adam Oravec)
9. *Kingdom*
10. *City of Fear*
11. *Birds of the Living Dead* - COMING SOON

Books of Judgment

1. *Sanderson of Metro* (with Bobby Nash)
2. *Serpent Rising* (with Greg Gick)
3. *Rising Son* (with Adam Oravec) - COMING SOON

SHORT STORY COLLECTIONS

The Wraith Vol. 1
The Wraith Vol. 2 - COMING SOON
Lance Star – Sky Ranger Vol. 1

NON-FICTION

The Hitchers of Oz
Beyond the Lens (edited)

www.glowingeyesmedia.com

THE BROKEN CHAIN

a George 'Magpie' Collins mystery #1

by

Len Driscoll

GLOWING EYES MEDIA
WOLLONGONG

GLOWING EYES MEDIA
PO Box 31
Wollongong NSW 2520

ISBN 978-0-646-72201-6

THE BROKEN CHAIN

PUBLISHED BY GLOWING EYES MEDIA, August 2025
www.glowingeyesmedia.com
FRONT COVER ART by Anon
COVER LAYOUT AND DESIGN AND INTERIOR DESIGN by Frank Dirscherl
EDITED by Claude Aylmer
FIRST EDITION

For more on *The Broken Chain*
visit www.glowingeyesmedia.com

Text set in Garamond-Normal. Printed and bound in the USA

NATIONAL LIBRARY OF AUSTRALIA

A catalogue record for this book is available from the National Library of Australia

For lovers of Chandler and MacDonald...this one's for you

THE BROKEN CHAIN

~ Chapter 1 ~

The woman came into my office like smoke drifting through a half-closed door. She was dressed in dove-grey from her felt hat to her kid gloves, and she moved with the careful precision of someone who'd learned early that the world was full of sharp edges.

It was a Thursday morning in late March, and Sydney was settling into autumn the way a tired man settles into his favorite chair. The heat had broken finally, and through my second-floor window on Castlereagh Street I could see office workers hurrying past in proper coats again, their faces turned away from the cool southerly that had been blowing for three days straight.

I'd been reading the *Herald* and working on my second cup of coffee when she knocked. The headline was something about the Labor Party's chances in the next election, and I was feeling cautiously optimistic about both the political situation and my bank balance. It had been a good month—a missing person case that ended happily, a simple adultery job that paid well, and a small matter involving some jewelry that had gone missing from a Woollahra mansion. The jewelry case had been particularly satisfying, since it turned out the owner's nephew had been systematically stealing from his aunt to pay gambling debts. I'd always had a soft spot for exposed bullies.

"Mr. Collins?" Her voice was cultured, with just a trace of something harder underneath—like good silver with a steel core. "I hope I'm not disturbing you."

"Not at all. Please, sit down." I gestured to the client chair across from my desk. It was a decent piece of furniture, mahogany with green leather padding, and it gave the office a respectable air that seemed to help with the better class of client. "What can I do for you?"

She settled into the chair with the fluid grace of someone who'd been taught how to move properly, then removed her gloves finger by finger with the kind of deliberate care that suggested she was buying time to think. Her hands were pale and long-fingered, with perfectly manicured nails. No wedding ring, but there was a thin band of lighter skin on her ring finger that suggested recent removal.

"My name is Isobel Latimer," she said, and the name meant something to me. The Latimers owned property all over Sydney, had interests in shipping and construction, and moved in the kind of circles where people didn't usually need private detectives. "I heard you used to be a criminal."

"'Used to be' being the operative description," I said.

"A thief?"

"I liked sparkly things, hence the nickname."

She looked at me like she didn't know what I was talking about.

"Magpie," I said, putting her out of her misery. "You've done your research. Now, are you going to tell me how I can help you, are we just going to reminisce about the good old days?"

"I believe you help people find things that are lost."

"People, mostly. Sometimes things. What exactly are you looking for, Miss Latimer?"

"Mrs. Latimer," she corrected gently. "Though I'm recently widowed." That explained the missing ring. "I'm looking for my brother. My adopted brother, actually. His name is Charlie Bristow."

I pulled out a notebook and uncapped my pen. "How long has he been missing?"

"Since Monday." She opened her purse—expensive leather, probably Italian—and extracted a silver cigarette case. Her fingers trembled slightly as she selected a cigarette. "He left our house in Potts Point on Monday evening and hasn't returned. The police..." She paused, the cigarette halfway to her lips. "The police don't seem particularly concerned. They say young men his age often disappear for a few days."

"How old is Charlie?"

"Nineteen." She lit the cigarette with a matching silver lighter, and I caught a glimpse of an engraved monogram: *I.L.* "But he's not the sort to simply vanish. He's quite responsible, actually. Works part-time keeping books for a shipping company, attends evening classes at the technical college. He has ambitions."

I studied her face as she spoke. She was probably in her early thirties, with the kind of pale beauty that suggested good breeding and careful maintenance. Her eyes were grey-green, the color of Sydney harbour on an overcast day, and they held secrets the way deep water holds sunken ships.

"Tell me about Monday evening. What was Charlie's mood? Did he say where he was going?"

She drew deeply on her cigarette, and for a moment her composed mask slipped. "He seemed... agitated. Excited, perhaps. He'd been asking questions lately about the family, about his adoption. We took him in when he was very young, you see. After his mother died."

"What kind of questions?"

"About his inheritance. Charlie seemed to believe his mother had left him something of value. A piece of jewelry, specifically." She paused, studying the ash on her cigarette. "He wasn't entirely wrong. There was a chain—a diamond chain—that had belonged to her. Nothing of great value, you understand, but it had sentimental worth. Charlie had been asking to see it."

"And did you show it to him?"

Another pause, longer this time. "Yes. On Monday afternoon. He seemed quite taken with it, asked many questions about where it had come from, whether there were other pieces. I'm afraid I couldn't answer most of his questions. The chain was simply something we'd kept in the family safe."

"Is the chain missing?"

Her hand went to her throat in an unconscious gesture. "I'm afraid so. When I checked the safe after Charlie disappeared, it was gone. I can only assume he took it with him."

I made notes, but something about her story felt off. Diamond chains that hold little to no monetary value. The tremor in her hands, the way she couldn't quite meet my eyes when she talked about the chain, the careful precision of her words—it all suggested someone who was editing the truth as she spoke.

"Mrs. Latimer, I have to ask this: is it possible Charlie simply took the chain and left town? Young men sometimes do impulsive things, especially when they feel they've been treated unfairly."

Her grey-green eyes flashed. "Charlie would never steal from family. Whatever his faults, he's an honorable boy. If he took the chain, it was because he believed it belonged to him."

"And you don't think it did?"

"I think," she said carefully, "that Charlie may have gotten some romantic notions about his mother and her circumstances. The chain was pretty, but it wasn't particularly valuable. Certainly not worth running away for."

The no-value diamond chain again. I leaned back in my chair. Outside, a tram clanged its way down Castlereagh Street, and I could hear the distant sound of construction work from one of the new buildings going up near Martin Place. The city was changing, growing, but some things remained constant—families with secrets, young men who asked too many questions, and the kind of small mysteries that turned out to be anything but small.

"What about the rest of your family? Does Charlie have any conflict with them?"

"My brother Dominic is...protective of family interests. He wasn't pleased when Charlie started asking questions about his inheritance. But he would never do anything to harm him." She said this with the conviction of someone trying to convince herself as much as me.

"I'll need to speak with your brother. And I'll need a photograph of Charlie, a list of his friends, places he might go. My rate is five pounds a day plus expenses."

She opened her purse again and counted out fifteen pounds onto my desk. "Will this be sufficient to start?"

"More than sufficient. But Mrs. Latimer, I should warn you—when young men disappear like this, they're usually running from something or toward something. Either way, you might not like what I find."

She stood and pulled on her gloves with the same careful precision she'd used to remove them. "Mr. Collins, I've lived in Sydney society for most of my adult life. I'm quite accustomed to not liking what I find."

After she left, I sat for a while looking at the money on my desk and thinking about trembling hands and diamond chains of no great value. In my experience, people didn't hire private detectives to find jewelry that wasn't worth much, and they didn't pay in advance unless they were either very rich or very desperate.

Isobel Latimer was probably both.

I locked the money in my desk drawer and reached for my hat. The NSW Masonic Club next door would be serving lunch soon, and I wanted to think about Charlie Bristow and valueless diamond chains over a decent steak and a beer. Sometimes the best way to understand a mystery was to let it percolate while you dealt with the simple, honest business of eating well.

But first, I had some phone calls to make. Tom Majors down at the police station might have some unofficial thoughts about missing young men and prominent families. And I had a feeling that before this case was over, I'd need all the unofficial help I could get.

The woman in grey had brought me more than a simple missing person case. She'd brought me the kind of trouble that started with trembling hands and ended with blood on the harbour.

I just didn't know it yet.

~ Chapter 2 ~

The smell of the harbour hit me before I saw it—salt and tar and the sweet corruption of things that had died in dark water. I'd taken the tram down to Circular Quay and walked east along the waterfront, past the ferry terminals and the fish markets, until I reached the maze of wharves and warehouses that stretched like broken fingers into Sydney harbour.

The union hall sat on Hickson Road like a brick fist thrown at the water. It was a squat, practical building with high windows and a red-painted door that had been kicked open so many times the hinges sagged. A hand-painted sign read "Maritime Workers Union—Sydney Branch" in letters that had once been white but were now the color of old bones.

I'd called Tom Majors before leaving my office, and he'd given me what he could about Charlie Bristow without asking too many questions, though I could tell he was holding something back. The boy had been seen at the union hall on Monday evening, talking to some of the older dockworkers. According to the beat constable who'd taken the initial missing person report, Charlie had been asking questions about the old days, about men who'd worked the docks during the war.

"Funny thing for a toff's adopted son to be interested in," Tom had said. "But then, funny things have a way of making sense once you dig deep enough."

The afternoon shift was changing as I approached the hall. Men in heavy coats and wool caps streamed out of the building, their faces weathered by wind and hard work. They moved with the loose-limbed gait of people who'd spent their lives lifting heavy things and knew how to save their strength for when it counted.

I pushed through the red door into a haze of cigarette smoke and the kind of masculine democracy that comes from shared hardship. The main room was lined with wooden benches and dominated by a small stage where union business was conducted. Propaganda posters covered the walls —calls for better wages, warnings about scab labor, and a large photograph of Ben Chifley looking stern and paternal.

The man behind the small bar in the corner was built like a brick shithouse and had the kind of face that suggested he'd been arguing with the world for about sixty years. He looked up as I approached, taking in my decent suit and clean hands with the practiced eye of someone who'd learned to sort people into categories quickly.

"You're not a docker," he said. It wasn't a question.

"No, I'm not. I'm looking for someone who might be able to help me with some information."

"What kind of information?"

"The kind that costs a drink and gets paid for with honest answers."

He almost smiled. "Fair enough. What are you drinking?"

"Beer will do fine."

He drew two schooners and slid one across the scarred wooden bar. "I'm Bill Murphy. I run this place when the officials aren't around to run it themselves. What's your name and what do you want to know?"

"George Collins. I'm a private inquiry agent. I'm looking for information about a young man named Charlie Bristow. He was here Monday evening."

Murphy's expression didn't change, but something shifted behind his eyes. "Charlie Bristow. That's the Latimer boy, isn't it? The adopted one."

"You know him?"

"I know of him. Word gets around. Young man with questions about the old days, about men who worked here during the war. Strange thing for someone from his background to be interested in." He sipped his beer thoughtfully. "You might want to talk to Big Sid. He was here Monday, had a good long chat with the boy."

"Where can I find Big Sid?"

"Right over there." Murphy nodded toward a corner table where a massive man sat alone, working his way through what looked like his third or fourth beer. "Sidney Brennan. Been working these docks for thirty years, knows every story worth knowing and a few that aren't."

I thanked Murphy and carried my beer across the room. Big Sid was appropriately named—he stood about six-foot-four and was built like a man who'd spent his life wrestling cargo nets and ship's lines. His left eye had a lazy drift to it, the result of some old injury, but his right eye was sharp and calculating.

"Sidney Brennan?"

"That's right. You're the private man Murphy called over. Sit down, have a drink. Always time for a beer when it's bought by someone with questions."

I settled into the chair across from him. "You talked to Charlie Bristow Monday evening."

"I did. Interesting young fellow. Polite, well-spoken, but with something eating at him. Like a dog with a bone it can't quite crack." Sid's good eye studied me carefully. "He was asking about the old days, about men who worked here during the war. Specific men."

"What kind of men?"

"The kind who didn't just work the docks. The kind who had other interests, other connections. Charlie was particularly interested in union business from around 1918, 1919. Kept asking about shipping manifests, about cargo that might have gone missing."

I leaned forward. "What was he looking for?"

"Well, that's the interesting question, isn't it? Charlie wasn't asking about general dock business. He was asking about specific people, specific connections. Kept mentioning a name—Mick Tierney. But more than that, he seemed to think there was something about his own family that he needed to understand."

"The Latimers?"

Sid drained his beer and signaled Murphy for another. "That's where it gets complicated. See, Charlie wasn't just asking about Tierney. He was asking about connections between Tierney and the Latimers. Like he thought there was some history there that nobody had told him about."

The name hit me like a slap. I'd heard of Mick Tierney, though I'd never had occasion to meet him. He'd been a union enforcer back in the day, the kind of man who settled disputes with his fists and asked questions later. After the war, he'd gone into business for himself—the kind of business that operated in the grey spaces between legal and illegal.

"What did you tell Charlie about Tierney?"

"I told him the truth. That Mick Tierney was a hard man in hard times, but that he'd left the union years ago. That if Charlie wanted to know more about him, he'd have to ask elsewhere." Sid's lazy eye seemed to focus on something over my shoulder. "But I also told him to be careful. Some stones are better left unturned."

"Did he listen to your advice?"

"Does any nineteen-year-old listen to advice from his elders?" Sid laughed, but there was no humor in it. "Charlie thanked me politely and left. But I got the feeling he was going to keep digging. Had that look about him, like a man who'd found something about his own family that didn't sit right."

I finished my beer and stood to leave. "If Charlie comes back, would you let me know? I'm trying to find him for his family."

"His family." Sid's voice was flat. "That would be the Latimers."

"That's right."

"Funny thing about families, Mr. Collins. Sometimes the people who claim to love you the most are the ones you should be most careful around." He looked up at me with both eyes focused for the first time. "Charlie Bristow may have been adopted by the Latimers, but he was asking questions like a man who thought there was something about his own past that didn't add up. Something the family maybe didn't want him to know."

I left the union hall with more questions than answers, but also with a clearer sense of what Charlie Bristow had been looking for. The boy hadn't simply run away with a diamond chain. He'd been investigating something about his own family, following connections between the Latimers and people like Mick Tierney that nobody had bothered to explain to him.

The afternoon was fading as I walked back along the waterfront. The harbour was settling into its evening rhythm —ferries carrying workers home, fishing boats heading out for the night catch, and the eternal dance of cargo ships and tugboats that kept the city's commerce flowing.

I stopped at a phone box near the Quay and called Tom Majors at police headquarters.

"Tom, it's George. I need to know what you can tell me about a man named Mick Tierney."

There was a pause. "Mick Tierney. Now that's a name I haven't heard in a while. What's your interest in him?"

"He's connected to the Bristow missing person case."

Tom's voice carried a note of warning. "Magpie, you might want to tread carefully there. The Latimers have friends in high places."

"What about Tierney?"

"Tierney's a different kind of problem. He was union muscle back in the day, but he's been running his own operation for years now. Import-export business, they call it. The kind where not all the imports and exports appear on the official manifests."

"Smuggling?"

"Among other things. Nothing we've ever been able to prove, but Tierney's the kind of man who always seems to have money when other people are struggling. He's got a warehouse operation down near Darling Harbour, keeps to himself mostly."

"Any connection to the Latimers?"

"Not that I know of. But if Charlie Bristow was asking questions about Tierney, he might have been walking into something bigger than he realized. Tierney's not the kind of man who appreciates curiosity."

I thanked Tom and hung up, then stood for a moment watching the evening traffic on George Street. The city was full of people heading home to their families, to their dinners and their quiet evening routines. But somewhere in this same city, Charlie Bristow was either hiding or being hidden, and a man named Mick Tierney was conducting business that didn't appear on official manifests.

I thought about Isobel Latimer's trembling hands and her careful explanation of the diamond chain's modest value. I thought about Big Sid's warning about stones better left unturned. And I thought about the way family secrets had a habit of spreading like poison through generations.

The case was becoming more complicated, but it was also becoming more interesting. Charlie Bristow hadn't just disappeared with a piece of jewelry. He'd disappeared while investigating something that connected his adoptive family to the shadowy world of wartime profiteering and union corruption.

Tomorrow, I'd pay a visit to the Latimer mansion in Potts Point. I wanted to meet Dominic Latimer and get a sense of what kind of man could raise an adopted son while keeping secrets that were worth killing for.

Because by now, I was beginning to suspect that Charlie Bristow wasn't just missing. He was in danger, and the danger came from the people who claimed to love him most.

The harbour wind was picking up, carrying the smell of rain and the promise of a storm. I turned my collar up and headed back toward the city, following the ghost of a nineteen-year-old boy who'd asked too many questions and found answers that somebody didn't want him to have.

~ Chapter 3 ~

The Latimer mansion crouched on the hill above Potts Point like a stone beast watching the harbour. It was one of those Victorian monuments to money and respectability that had been built when Sydney was young and optimistic, before the city learned that some fortunes came with blood on them.

I'd taken the tram up from Circular Quay, past the neat terraces of Elizabeth Bay and into the rarefied air where Sydney's old money lived in careful isolation from the world that had made them rich. The morning was crisp and clear, with the kind of autumn light that made the harbour sparkle like scattered diamonds.

The house sat behind iron gates and a hedge that had been trimmed to military precision. It was built of sandstone that had weathered to the color of old bones, with bay windows that looked out over the water and a wraparound verandah that suggested leisurely afternoons and the kind of conversations that never quite said what they meant.

I pushed through the gate and walked up a gravel drive lined with plane trees. The front door was solid timber painted black, with brass fittings that had been polished to a mirror shine. A brass nameplate read "Latimer" in elegant script.

The woman who answered my knock was small and neat, with the kind of face that suggested she'd been pretty once but had traded beauty for efficiency somewhere along the way. She wore a grey dress with a white collar and looked at me with the practiced wariness of someone who'd spent years protecting her employers from unwanted visitors.

"I'm George Collins," I said, handing her my card. "Mrs. Latimer is expecting me."

She studied the card with the concentration of someone who couldn't quite read but didn't want to admit it. "I'll see if Mrs. Latimer is receiving visitors. Please wait here."

She left me standing in a foyer that had been designed to impress. The ceiling was fifteen feet high, with elaborate plasterwork that must have cost more than most people earned in a year. Oil paintings lined the walls—landscapes and portraits of stern-faced men in military uniforms. A grandfather clock ticked in the corner with the kind of measured authority that came from Swiss precision and English money.

"Mr. Collins." The voice came from the top of a curved staircase that swept down from the second floor like something out of a stage set. The man descending it moved with the casual arrogance of someone who'd never had to worry about whether he belonged somewhere.

Dominic Latimer, presumably, was probably in his early forties, tall and lean with the kind of good looks that came from careful breeding and regular exercise. His hair was dark with distinguished touches of grey at the temples, and his eyes were the same grey-green as his sister's but harder, like stones that had been polished by years of getting what they wanted.

"I'm Dominic Latimer," he said, confirming his identity and extending a hand that was soft but strong. "Isobel mentioned you might be coming by. Something about young Charlie, I understand."

"That's right. I'm trying to trace his movements on Monday evening. I was hoping to see his room, talk to anyone who might have seen him before he left."

Dominic's smile was the kind that never quite reached his eyes. "I'm afraid Charlie's room won't tell you much. The boy was always secretive about his affairs. But you're welcome to look, of course. Anything that might help bring him home."

He led me up the staircase, past more portraits and into a hallway lined with doors. The carpet was thick enough to muffle footsteps, and the walls were covered with fabric that probably cost more per yard than most people spent on clothes.

"Charlie's room is at the end of the hall," Dominic said. "He preferred the privacy, always claimed he needed quiet to study. Though I suspect he used the isolation for other purposes."

"What kind of purposes?"

"The kind that young men get up to when they think no one is watching." Dominic's voice carried a note of casual contempt. "Charlie had romantic notions about his origins, about his place in the world. I'm afraid we may have indulged him too much."

The room at the end of the hall was smaller than I'd expected, with a narrow bed and a desk positioned under a window that looked out over the back garden. It was neat in the way that suggested someone had cleaned it recently, but there was something wrong with the scene.

The window was broken.

Not shattered dramatically, but cracked in a spider web pattern that suggested something had hit it from the inside. The glass was still in place, held together by some kind of tape that had been applied with care.

"What happened to the window?" I asked.

Dominic glanced at it with the kind of studied indifference that suggested he'd been expecting the question. "Charlie had a bit of a tantrum before he left. Threw something at the glass, I'm told. We haven't had time to repair it properly."

I examined the window more closely. The crack pattern was wrong for something thrown from inside—it looked more like something had hit it from outside, or like pressure had been applied to the glass in a way that suggested violence.

"Mind if I look around a bit?"

"Be my guest. Though I doubt you'll find much. Charlie was quite thorough in cleaning out his personal effects before he left."

That was interesting. In my experience, people who were running away in a panic didn't usually take time to tidy up their rooms. There were a few photos of a young man—Charlie himself I assumed—arranged on his desk. I started going through the desk drawers, but they were empty except for a few pencils and some school notebooks. The wardrobe held a few items of clothing, but nothing that suggested a young man's personality or interests.

I was about to give up when I noticed something tucked behind the desk—a small piece of paper that had fallen and caught in the narrow space between the furniture and the wall. I worked it free and smoothed it out.

It was a fragment of a photograph, torn roughly from a larger picture. The image showed three children—two boys and a girl—standing in front of what looked like the same house I was in now. The children were younger versions of Dominic and Isobel Latimer, but there was a third child, a boy who looked to be about five years old.

But it was the figure in the background that caught my attention. A woman stood behind the children, partially obscured by shadow, but clearly present. She was young, with dark hair and a face that had been beautiful before whatever had happened to put fear in her eyes.

"Interesting photograph," I said, holding it up.

Dominic's mask slipped for just a moment, and I caught a glimpse of something that might have been anger or might have been fear. "I have no idea what that is. Probably just some old family photograph that got damaged."

"The woman in the background—who is she?"

"I couldn't say. We've had many servants over the years. They come and go." His voice was steady, but his hands had clenched into fists. "Is there anything else you need to see, Mr. Collins? I have business to attend to."

I pocketed the photograph fragment. "Just a couple more questions. Do you know a man named Mick Tierney?"

The change in Dominic's expression was subtle but unmistakable. "I know of him. He's some sort of businessman, I believe. Import-export. Why do you ask?"

"Charlie was asking questions about him on Monday evening. I thought there might be a connection."

"I can't imagine what connection there would be. The Latimers don't associate with men like Tierney." The contempt in his voice was real, but there was something else underneath it—something that might have been worry.

"What about during the war? Any business connections then?"

"Mr. Collins, I think you may be confusing us with someone else. The Latimer family has always been quite particular about our associations." He moved toward the door with the kind of measured step that suggested he was working to control his temper. "I'm afraid I really must ask you to leave now. If you have any further questions, you can contact our solicitor."

I followed him back down the staircase, and he escorted me to the front door with a huff of petulance.

The neat little maid appeared as if summoned and showed me out. I thanked her and left, but I didn't go far. Instead, I walked around to the side of the house where Charlie's window faced the back garden.

The garden was formal and well-maintained, with hedges cut into geometric shapes and gravel paths that led to a small greenhouse. But what interested me was the area directly under Charlie's window. The ground was soft earth, recently turned, and there were footprints in it—not the kind made by a gardener, but the kind made by someone who'd been standing there looking up at the window.

I knelt and examined the prints more closely. They were made by expensive shoes, the kind that Dominic Latimer might wear. But there was something else in the soft earth—a small piece of glass that had fallen from the window above.

The glass was clean on one side but had blood on the other.

I wrapped the glass fragment in my handkerchief and stood up, brushing dirt from my knees. The broken window, the footprints, the blood—they painted a picture that was very different from Dominic's story about Charlie throwing a tantrum before he left. It didn't equal murder, necesarilly, but it did point to violence of some sort.

It looked more like someone had been standing outside Charlie's window, and that someone had been hurt in the process of whatever had happened there.

I walked back to the front of the house and stood for a moment looking up at the Victorian mansion with its careful facade and its hidden secrets. The Latimers had money and respectability, but they also had connections to people like Mick Tierney that they didn't want to acknowledge.

Charlie Bristow had discovered that connection, and now he was missing. The question was whether he'd run away to escape the truth he'd uncovered, or whether someone had made sure he couldn't share it.

The fragment of photograph in my pocket showed a woman who'd been young and beautiful and afraid. I was beginning to suspect that she held the key to understanding Charlie's investigation into his own family's past.

But first, I needed to know more about Mick Tierney and his connection to the Latimer family. And I needed to find out what Charlie had discovered about the woman in the photograph—the woman whose presence had been carefully edited out of the family's official history.

The harbour wind was picking up again, carrying the smell of rain and the promise of more storms to come. I pulled my coat tighter and headed back toward the city, following the trail of a missing boy who'd asked too many questions about the past.

Behind me, the Latimer mansion settled back into its careful silence, keeping its secrets the way old houses keep their ghosts—hidden but never quite gone.

~ Chapter 4 ~

The NSW Police Headquarters on Phillip Street was one of those solid sandstone buildings that the colonial government had built to last forever. It squatted between the courts and the treasury like a promise that law and order would outlive the politicians who paid for it. The morning sun caught the windows and turned them into mirrors that reflected the city's ambitions back at itself.

I'd known Tom Majors for eight years, ever since he'd caught me with a handful of stolen emeralds and decided I was more useful as an informant than as a prisoner. It was Tom who'd helped me go straight, who'd vouched for me when I applied for my private inquiry license, and who'd occasionally bent the rules when a case required the kind of knowledge that came from having walked on both sides of the law. He was also one of the very few people to still call me by my nickname.

The desk sergeant recognized me and waved me through without the usual bureaucratic dance. I found Tom in his office on the second floor, hunched over a stack of reports with the kind of concentration that suggested he was trying to make sense of something that didn't want to be understood.

"Magpie." He looked up and smiled, but there was something tired in his expression. "I was wondering when you'd turn up. Heard you visited the Latimer house."

"Word travels fast."

"In this city, it does. Especially when it involves prominent families." He gestured to the chair across from his desk. "Coffee?"

"Black, thanks."

Tom poured two cups from a pot that looked like it had been brewing since the Boer War. The coffee was strong enough to wake the dead and bitter enough to make them wish they'd stayed buried, but it was hot and it was free.

"Tell me more about Charlie Bristow," I said. "You were pretty reticent the last time I asked you."

Tom leaned back in his chair and studied me with the kind of look that suggested he was deciding how much truth I could handle. "You're poking a stick into a snake pit, mate. You know that, don't you?"

"I'm getting that impression. What kind of snakes are we talking about?"

"The kind that have money and connections and don't like having their business discussed in public." He sighed, then opened a file drawer and pulled out a thin folder. "I had a look at the boy's background after you called yesterday. Interesting reading."

He slid the folder across the desk. Inside was a collection of official documents—birth certificates, adoption papers, school records—the paper trail that followed every citizen from cradle to grave. But there were gaps in the record, places where information should have been but wasn't. And no photograph of his mother. A thought had occurred to me. The woman in the photograph fragment...was she Charlie's mother?

"Charlie Bristow," Tom said, "born 1916, mother deceased 1918, or so we're supposed to believe. Adopted by the Latimer family the same year. Father unknown."

"What happened to the mother? You doubt she died?"

"That's where it gets interesting. There's a death certificate and it says she died of influenza. But there's no record of where she's buried, no next of kin listed except for Charlie himself. It's like she existed just long enough to have a baby and then vanished from the world. Is she dead? Maybe, maybe not."

I studied the documents more closely. The adoption papers were signed by a judge who'd been dead for ten years, and the witness signatures were illegible. "This looks like it was arranged quietly."

"Very quietly. The kind of arrangement that requires favors and involves people who prefer not to have their names associated with certain activities." Tom sipped his coffee and grimaced. "Magpie, I'm going to tell you something that doesn't leave this room. The Latimers aren't just another wealthy family. They've got connections that go back to the war, to deals that were made when the government needed things done and didn't ask too many questions about how they got done."

"What kind of deals?"

"The kind that involve shipping manifests that don't match cargo manifests, and cargo that disappears between the wharf and the warehouse. The kind that make fortunes for people who know how to keep their mouths shut."

I thought about the diamond chain that Isobel Latimer had described as being of no great value, and about Charlie's investigation into his family's past. "You think Charlie found out about these deals?"

"I think it likely he found out something that made him dangerous to people who've spent a lot of money making sure certain things stay buried." Tom closed the file and looked at me seriously. "The boy's mother—her name was Margaret Bristow. Born to the pink, or so we're told, but her family reportedly came down in the world just prior to the war, forcing young Margaret into service. She worked as a housemaid for the Latimers during the war. Young woman, pretty, the kind who might catch the eye of someone she shouldn't have been involved with."

Born to the pink. That would explain how a simple housemaid would come to own a diamond chain.

"Someone like Dominic Latimer?"

"That's not in the official record. But if you read between the lines, it suggests possibilities that certain people would prefer not to have discussed."

I finished my coffee and stood up. "Tom, I need to ask you something, and I need you to be straight with me. If Charlie Bristow turns up dead, will there be a real investigation?"

Tom was quiet for a long moment, staring at the file on his desk. When he looked up, his expression was grim. "Magpie, I've been a policeman for twenty-three years. I've seen cases that got solved and cases that got buried. The Latimers have friends in high places, and those friends have long memories."

"That's not an answer."

"It's the only answer I can give you." He stood and walked to the window, looking out at the city that sprawled below us. "But I will tell you this—if something happens to that boy, and if you can bring me evidence that doesn't depend on the cooperation of people who'd rather see it disappear, then I'll do what I can to see that justice gets done."

It was more than I'd expected and less than I'd hoped for. But it was Tom's way of telling me that I was on my own, that whatever I found would have to be ironclad before the law would be willing to act on it.

I left police headquarters with more questions than answers, but also with a clearer picture of what Charlie Bristow had been up against. The boy hadn't just been investigating his family's past—he'd come across a conspiracy that involved likely wartime profiteering, illegal adoptions, and the kind of people who solved problems by making them disappear.

The diamond chain that Isobel Latimer had described as worthless was probably part of a hidden inheritance, something that had belonged to Charlie's mother and represented a claim on the Latimer fortune that nobody wanted to acknowledge. Charlie had discovered the truth about his parentage, and that truth was dangerous enough to want to kill for.

I walked back toward Castlereagh Street, thinking about young women who died of influenza and left no trace of their existence, about adoption papers that had been signed by dead judges, and about the kind of favours that people in power did for each other when the stakes were high enough.

The city moved around me with its usual rhythm—trams and automobiles, office workers and shopkeepers, all of them going about their daily business while secrets from the war years festered like old wounds that wouldn't heal. Sydney was a city built on ambition and opportunity, but it was also a city where the powerful protected their own and the weak disappeared without leaving ripples.

The photograph fragment in my desk drawer showed a woman who'd been young and beautiful and afraid. I felt sure it was Margaret Bristow, Charlie's mother, who'd worked as a housemaid and apparently died of influenza in 1918. But the fear in her eyes suggested that she'd known something was going to happen to her, and that her death might not have been as natural as the official records claimed.

I decided to head back to the wharves to press Big Sid for more information. If Charlie had been digging into the family's past, he would have needed a base of operations, somewhere he could work without the Latimers watching his every move. Sid might know more than he'd let on during our first conversation.

As evening approached, I locked up the office and walked to the harbour. The docks were quieter now, with only a few late workers finishing their shifts. I found Big Sid at the union hall, nursing a beer and reading a newspaper by the light of a kerosene lamp.

"Collins," he said without looking up. "Heard you paid a visit to the Latimer place today. How'd that go?"

"Interesting. Tell me something, Sid—where was Charlie staying while he was asking his questions about the family?"

Sid's good eye focused on me with sharp intelligence. "You think the boy's in real trouble, don't you?"

"I think he found something that certain people would prefer stayed buried. And I think those people are willing to go to considerable lengths to keep their secrets."

Sid was quiet for a moment, then folded his newspaper and set it aside. "Charlie was staying in one of the boarding houses in Woolloomooloo. Near the fish markets. I saw him coming and going, always looking over his shoulder like he expected someone to follow him."

"You know which boarding house?"

"Mrs. Kowalski's place. Old Polish woman, runs a tight ship but doesn't ask too many questions." He paused. "Collins, that boy was scared. Not just worried scared, but the kind of scared that comes from knowing someone wants to hurt you."

I thanked Sid and left the union hall with a new lead to follow. Charlie had been using a boarding house as his base while he investigated his family's past. If I could find something there where he'd been staying, I might be able to discover what he'd learned about the Latimer family's connection to Mick Tierney.

The harbour wind was picking up again, carrying the promise of rain and the smell of secrets that had been hidden too long. I pulled my coat tighter and headed toward Woolloomooloo, following the trail of a missing boy who'd asked too many questions about the past.

The stakes were getting higher, and the people involved were getting more dangerous. But I'd made a promise to Isobel Latimer, and more importantly, I'd made a promise to myself. Charlie Bristow deserved justice, and his mother deserved to have her story told.

Even if that story brought down one of Sydney's most prominent families.

~ Chapter 5 ~

The boarding house in Woolloomooloo squatted between a fishmonger's shop and a pawn broker like a guilty secret trying to hide in plain sight. The smell of rotting fish and yesterday's cooking hung in the air like a fog that no amount of harbour breeze could clear. It was the kind of place where people went when they'd run out of better options, or when they needed to disappear from the world for a while.

After Big Sid's lead, a further few discrete inquiries and a couple of pound notes had led me right to Mrs. Kowalski's establishment, where Charlie had been registered under the name Charles Brown. It was the kind of obvious alias that suggested either panic or inexperience, and probably both.

The woman who answered my knock was somewhere between forty and death, with the kind of weathered face that came from too much gin and too little sleep. Her grey hair was pulled back in a bun that had given up trying to be neat, and her dress was the color of old dishwater.

"Mrs. Kowalski?" I showed her my license. "I'm George Collins. I'm looking for information about one of your tenants—Charles Brown."

She looked at my license with the kind of suspicion that suggested she'd had dealings with the law before and hadn't enjoyed the experience. "What's he done?"

"Nothing that I know of. His family's worried about him. He's been missing for a few days."

"Missing?" She laughed, but there was no humor in it. "Charlie ain't missing. He's just scared. Been jumping at shadows ever since that man came to see him."

"What man?"

"Big fellow, Irish accent. Looked like he could break a man's neck with his bare hands." She wiped her hands on her apron and stepped aside. "You'd better come in. Standing on the doorstep ain't good for business."

The interior of the boarding house was as depressing as the exterior promised. The wallpaper was peeling in places, and the carpet had seen better decades. The air was thick with the smell of boiled cabbage and human desperation.

"Charlie took the room at the back," she said, leading me down a narrow hallway lined with doors. "Paid a week in advance, cash. Said he was between situations and needed a quiet place to think."

"When did the other man visit?"

"Tuesday morning. Early, before most of the tenants were awake. I heard voices through the walls—Charlie's and this other fellow's. Sounded like they were arguing about something."

We stopped at a door marked with a brass number 7. Mrs. Kowalski produced a key from her apron pocket and unlocked it. "Charlie cleared out Tuesday afternoon. Left most of his things but took his satchel and whatever money he had. Said he was going away for a while."

The room was small and spare, with a narrow bed, a washstand, and a window that looked out onto an alley where cats fought over scraps from the fishmonger's shop. Charlie's belongings were scattered around—clothes, books, a few personal items that suggested a young man trying to make sense of his place in the world.

"Tell me about the argument," I said, examining the contents of the washstand. There was a razor, a brush, and a small mirror that had been cracked down the middle.

"Couldn't make out all the words, but I heard the Irish fellow say something about a chain. Said it didn't belong to Charlie, that he should give it back before people got hurt."

I looked up from the mirror. "What did Charlie say?"

"He said the chain was his by right, that it had belonged to his mother. Said he wasn't giving it back to people who'd stolen it in the first place." She paused, remembering. "Then the Irish fellow said something about someone called Tierney, how Charlie didn't understand what he was dealing with."

Mick Tierney. The name kept coming up like a bad penny. I continued searching the room, looking for anything that might tell me where Charlie had gone or what he'd discovered about his family's past.

In the bottom drawer of the washstand, I found a bundle of letters tied with string. They were old, yellowed with age, and written in a woman's careful handwriting. The return address was a rooming house in Darlinghurst, and they were addressed to "My Dearest Charlie."

I untied the string and read the first letter. It was dated 1917, and it was from a woman named Margaret to someone she called "my sweet boy." The letter was full of the kind of tender words that a mother might write to a child, but there was something else underneath—a sense of urgency, of time running out.

"Mrs. Kowalski," I said, holding up the letters. "Did Charlie ever mention anything about his mother?"

"Not much. Said the family he lived with now were his family but also weren't. None of it made any sense to me." She looked at the letters with curious eyes. "One thing I do know is he spent a lot of time reading those letters, especially at night when he couldn't sleep."

Not much of what she told me made much sense to me, either, but it was clear she was a busybody of the highest order. Useful in my profession.

I read through several more letters, and a picture began to emerge. Margaret Bristow had been young and frightened, writing to a child she might never see again. The letters spoke of hidden things, of money that had been put aside for Charlie's future, of a chain that had been passed down through generations of women in her family.

The last letter was different. It was shorter, more urgent, and it was dated just days before Margaret's death in 1918. In it, she wrote about hiding something valuable, about making sure Charlie would be provided for if anything happened to her. She mentioned a name—Mick Tierney—and said that he would know where to find what belonged to Charlie.

"Mrs. Kowalski," I said, folding the letters carefully. "When Charlie left on Tuesday, did he say anything about where he was going?"

"He said he was going to find the truth, that he was tired of living a lie." She looked at me with eyes that had seen too much of the world's cruelty. "Mr. Collins, that boy was scared. Not just worried scared, but the kind of scared that comes from knowing someone wants to hurt you."

I thanked her and left the boarding house with more questions than answers. Charlie had been using the room as a base while he investigated his family's past. He'd found letters from his mother that mentioned Mick Tierney and a hidden inheritance. And Charlie likely had the valueless chain.

And now Charlie was missing.

I walked through the narrow streets of Woolloomooloo, past the terraces where working families lived in conditions that were better than the boarding house but not by much. The harbour was close here, close enough to smell the salt and hear the sounds of ships loading and unloading at the wharves.

The sun was starting to set, painting the sky in shades of orange and red that reflected off the water like scattered coins. I was thinking about Margaret Bristow's letters, about the fear in her words and the love that had survived even through death, when I noticed the footsteps behind me.

They'd been there for several blocks, matching my pace but staying far enough back to avoid notice. Two sets of footsteps, both heavy, both belonging to men who knew how to walk quietly when they needed to.

I turned down a side street that led toward the harbour, where the streetlights were farther apart and the shadows deeper. The footsteps followed, and I knew that whatever was about to happen, it would happen soon.

The alley I chose was narrow and dark, with high walls on both sides and only one way out. It was the kind of place where a man could disappear without anyone seeing or hearing what had happened to him. But it was also the kind of place where a man who knew how to take care of himself could even the odds.

I stopped walking and turned around.

There were two of them, both wearing dark trench coats and hats pulled low over their faces. They were big men, the kind who solved problems with their fists and didn't ask many questions about why the problems needed solving.

"Evening, gentlemen," I said, keeping my voice casual. "Lovely night for a walk."

The one on the left stepped forward. He had the kind of face that suggested he'd been in more fights than he'd won, with a nose that had been broken at least twice and scar tissue around his eyes.

"You're Collins," he said. It wasn't a question.

"That's right. And you are?"

"Someone who's here to give you some friendly advice." His voice carried the kind of Irish accent that Mrs. Kowalski had described. "You're poking around in business that doesn't concern you. That's not healthy."

"I'm a curious man by nature. It's an occupational hazard."

The second man moved to my right, trying to flank me. He was younger than his partner, with the kind of nervous energy that suggested he was new to this kind of work. His hand kept moving toward his coat pocket, where the outline of a weapon was visible.

"The advice is simple," the first man continued. "Stop asking questions about Charlie Bristow. Stop asking questions about Mick Tierney. Stop asking questions about chains and families and things that happened a long time ago."

"And if I don't?"

"Then you'll find out what happened to people who don't listen to friendly advice."

I let my hand drift toward my own coat pocket, where I kept a blackjack that had served me well in the years when I'd lived on the wrong side of the law. "Before I decide whether to take your advice, I'd like to know something. Where's Charlie Bristow?"

The two men exchanged glances. The younger one was getting more nervous, his hand moving closer to his weapon. The older one was calculating, trying to decide whether words would be enough or whether they'd need to use force.

"None of your business," he said finally. "Now you need to mind yours."

"That's not an answer."

"It's the only answer you're going to get." He stepped closer, and I could smell tobacco and whiskey on his breath. "Stay away from Tierney, Collins. The chain doesn't belong to the kid. It belongs to people who know how to take care of problems."

"What people?"

But I'd pushed too far. The younger man's nerve broke, and his hand went for his pocket. I moved faster, bringing the blackjack out in a smooth arc that caught him across the wrist. He cried out and stumbled backward, his weapon clattering to the ground.

The older man charged, and we went down in a tangle of arms and legs. He was strong, but I'd learned to fight in places where losing meant more than just a bruised ego. I got a knee into his stomach and rolled away, coming up in a crouch.

"You made a mistake, Collins," he gasped, pulling himself to his feet. "This isn't over."

"It is for tonight," I said, keeping the blackjack visible. "And next time you want to have a conversation, try knocking on my office door. I'm usually in."

They gathered themselves and their fallen weapon and disappeared into the darkness, leaving me alone in the alley with the smell of fear and violence hanging in the air like smoke.

I walked back toward the main street, thinking about what I'd learned. Whether Charlie Bristow was alive or not remained an open question. If he was, he was likely being held by people who considered him a problem to be solved, not a person to be protected. But it was a big if as far as I was concerned.

The chain that Isobel Latimer had described as worthless was valuable enough to motivate kidnapping and threats of violence. And Mick Tierney appeared to be at the center of it all, the man who'd known Charlie's mother and who possibly had some claim on the inheritance she'd left for her son. It was a stretch, I admitted, but the dots were still too far apart to join properly together right now.

I stopped at a phone box and called Tom Majors at home. He answered on the third ring, his voice thick with sleep.

"Tom, it's George. I need to ask you something, and I need you to be careful how you answer."

"What's wrong?"

"I just had a conversation with two men who tried to warn me off the case. They mentioned Mick Tierney, and they made it clear that people who ask too many questions about chains and families tend to have accidents."

There was a long pause. "Magpie, I told you this was a snake pit. Are you all right?"

"I'm fine. But I need to know—if something happens to me, will you make sure the right people know about the Latimer family and their connection to Tierney?"

"Nothing's going to happen to you. But yes, I'll make sure the right people know." His voice was grim. "Listen to me...maybe it's time to step back from this one. Some cases aren't worth dying for."

"This one is, Tom. There's a boy out there who's in trouble because he asked questions about his own family. That's not something I can walk away from."

I hung up and walked back to my office, thinking about Margaret Bristow's letters and the love that had survived even through death. Charlie had been looking for the truth about his past, and he'd found it. But the truth was dangerous to people who'd spent years keeping it buried.

The chain was more than just a piece of jewelry—it was a symbol of a connection that certain people wanted to deny. And Charlie Bristow was paying the price for trying to claim what was rightfully his.

But if they thought a couple of hired thugs would be enough to scare me off, they'd made a serious miscalculation. I'd tangled with worse than Mick Tierney in my time, and I'd learned that bullies only understood one kind of language.

The harbour wind was picking up again, carrying the promise of rain and the smell of secrets that had been hidden too long. I pulled my coat tighter and headed home, planning my next move in a game where the stakes were getting higher and the players were getting more dangerous.

If he was still alive, Charlie Bristow was out there somewhere, probably scared and alone, trusting that someone would come looking for him. I'd made a promise to his sister, but more than that, I'd made a promise to myself.

Some promises were worth keeping, no matter what the cost.

~ Chapter 6 ~

The NSW Masonic Club occupied a solid sandstone building next to my office on Castlereagh Street, its Art Deco Georgian facade giving nothing away about the mysteries that supposedly lay within. I'd eaten breakfast–and countless other meals–there over the years–I'd done the secretary a favour some years back and been allowed entry ever since–but I'd never paid much attention to the membership or the conversations that took place at the oak-paneled tables where Sydney's establishment gathered to discuss business over eggs and bacon. This morning was different.

I was looking for Abe Kerrigan, a former dockworker who'd parlayed his union connections into a comfortable retirement and a membership in one of the city's most exclusive clubs. Tom Majors had once mentioned Kerrigan's name in passing–a man who knew where the bodies were buried and who might be willing to talk if approached the right way. I thought he may have something for me and asked Tom to arrange a meeting.

I found him in the club's main dining room, a portly man in his sixties with the kind of face that suggested he'd spent more time laughing than worrying. He was working his way through a plate of kippers and reading the morning paper with the deliberate care of someone who had all the time in the world.

"Mr. Kerrigan?" I approached his table with the careful respect that the club's atmosphere demanded. "I'm George Collins. I believe Tom Majors mentioned I might be in touch."

Kerrigan looked up from his paper and studied me with sharp blue eyes that seemed to catalog everything they saw. "Ah, the private inquiry man. Tom said you were asking questions about the Latimer family."

"Among other things. I was hoping you might have a few minutes to talk."

"Sit down, Collins. Order yourself some breakfast. A man shouldn't discuss serious business on an empty stomach."

I signaled the waiter and ordered black coffee and toast. The club's dining room was filling up with the morning crowd—lawyers, doctors, businessmen, and retired civil servants who'd earned their place at the table through years of service to the city's power structure.

"Tom tells me you're looking into the disappearance of young Charlie Bristow," Kerrigan said, cutting into his kipper with surgical precision. "Interesting timing, that."

"Why interesting?"

"Because Charlie's been asking questions about things that happened during the war. And there are people who'd prefer those questions not be answered." He paused to sip his tea.

"You know anything about the Latimer family's business dealings during the war years?"

"I know they made money. Beyond that, I'm working on educated guesses." Kerrigan laughed, a sound like stones rolling in a barrel. "Educated guesses. That's diplomatic. The truth is, Collins, the Latimers made a fortune during the war, and they didn't do it by selling biscuits to the troops."

The waiter brought my coffee and toast. I waited until he was out of earshot before responding. "What kind of business were they in?"

"Import-export, officially. But there was always more cargo leaving the docks than appeared on the shipping manifests. And there was always more money in the Latimer accounts than could be explained by their legitimate business."

"You're talking about smuggling."

"I'm talking about a complicated arrangement that involved government contracts, union cooperation, and the kind of paperwork that disappeared when it became inconvenient." Kerrigan's voice was casual, but his eyes were watchful. "During the war, the government needed things done quickly and quietly. They didn't ask too many questions about methods as long as the results were satisfactory."

War profiteering, as I had surmised earlier. I then thought about the photograph fragment I'd found in Charlie's room, about the woman who'd been beautiful and afraid. "Where did the union fit into this arrangement?"

"The union provided the muscle when muscle was needed. And the union provided the silence when silence was required." Kerrigan finished his kipper and pushed the plate away. "There was a special fund, you see. Called it a charity fund, for the families of workers who'd been killed or injured. Very noble purpose, very worthy cause."

"But that's not what it was really for."

"Oh, it helped some families, certainly. But most of the money went to other purposes. Payments to people who needed to be convinced to look the other way. Investments in businesses that didn't exist. And sometimes, payments to people who needed to disappear."

The dining room was getting noisier as more members arrived for their morning routines. I leaned closer to Kerrigan, keeping my voice low. "You're saying the Latimers were involved in murder."

"I'm saying the Latimers were involved in a lot of things that required careful handling. And sometimes, when people became inconvenient, arrangements were made." He signaled the waiter for more tea. "The charity fund was administered by the union, but the real decisions were made by people who never got their hands dirty."

"People like Dominic Latimer."

"People like Dominic Latimer's father. Dominic was just a boy during the war, but he inherited the family business and all the obligations that came with it."

I sipped my coffee, thinking about the implications. "What kind of obligations?"

"The kind that involve offshore accounts and jewels that were never declared to the customs authorities. The kind that involve people who know where the money came from and expect to be paid for their silence." Kerrigan's voice was matter-of-fact, as if he were discussing the weather. "The charity fund was supposed to be temporary, something that would disappear when the war ended. But some arrangements have a way of becoming permanent."

"You're talking about blackmail."

"I'm talking about business relationships that became complicated over time. The union had records, you see.

Names, dates, amounts. The kind of information that could be embarrassing if it fell into the wrong hands."

A piece of the puzzle clicked into place. "Mick Tierney."

"Ah, you know about Tierney." Kerrigan's expression became more cautious. "Now there's a man who understood the value of information. Started as a union enforcer, but he had bigger ambitions. He saw the opportunities that the war created and made himself useful to the right people."

"What kind of opportunities?"

"The kind that involved moving valuable things from one place to another without too many questions being asked. Tierney had contacts in the shipping industry, and he knew how to make cargo disappear and reappear when necessary." Kerrigan paused as the waiter refilled his teacup. "But Tierney was also smart enough to keep records. Insurance, you might say."

I thought about the letters I'd found in Charlie's room, about Margaret Bristow's references to money that had been hidden for her son's future. "What happened to the money in the charity fund?"

"Officially, it was dissolved after the war. The books were audited, the accounts were closed, and everyone involved received commendations for their patriotic service." Kerrigan's smile was cynical. "Unofficially, a lot of money found its way into private accounts. Some of it legitimate profit, some of it less so."

"And some of it belonged to people who died before they could claim it."

"You're a quick study, Collins. Yes, some of the money was earmarked for people who didn't survive the war. Or who died shortly after it ended." He looked at me meaningfully. "There were quite a few cases of influenza in 1918, if you recall."

The implication was clear. Margaret Bristow had died not from influenza, but because she'd known too much about the charity fund and the arrangements that had been made in its name. And now her son was asking questions that threatened to expose the same secrets. "Where would records of this fund be kept?" I asked.

"The union records were supposedly destroyed years ago. But men like Latimer or Tierney don't destroy things that have value. They hide them." Kerrigan finished his tea and checked his pocket watch. "If such records still exist, they'd be in a place that's secure but accessible. Somewhere that people like them could get to them if he needed to, but where they wouldn't be found by accident."

"Any suggestions?"

"Well, if I were hiding something valuable, I'd want it to be in a place that looked respectable but had good security. Somewhere that important people went regularly, but where not everyone was welcome." He stood up, adjusting his waistcoat. "This club has excellent security, for instance. Thick walls, discrete staff, and the kind of membership that values privacy."

He was telling me something without saying it directly. The Masonic Club itself, or somewhere similar, might be where Dominic or Tierney—or both—had hidden their dirty laundry.

"Mr. Kerrigan," I said as he prepared to leave, "why are you telling me this?"

"Because Charlie Bristow deserves better than to disappear like his mother did. And because some secrets have been kept too long." He picked up his newspaper and tucked it under his arm. "Be careful, Collins. The people you're dealing with have been playing this game for a long time, and they don't like to lose. But if you insist on continuing...you might like to call on Clara Latimer."

"Clara...?" I had heard some vague mention of Dominic's wife at some point in my life, but nothing more than that. Kerrigan's statement proved eye-opening. He raised an eyebrow at me before he turned and walked away.

I sat alone at the table after he left, finishing my coffee and thinking about what I'd learned. The Latimer family's wealth was built on wartime profiteering and smuggling, with the cooperation of union officials like Tierney. A charity fund had been used to hide money and pay for silence. Margaret Bristow had died because she'd known too much, and now her son was missing for the same reason. But there were records somewhere, evidence that could expose the entire conspiracy. And if Kerrigan was right, those records were hidden in a place that was secure but accessible, respectable but discrete.

I thought about what Kerrigan had said about hiding something valuable in a place that was secure but accessible, respectable but discrete. Buildings like the Masonic Club had been used for all sorts of purposes during the war—storage, meetings, even temporary holding areas for sensitive materials. If Dominic or Tierney had needed a place to hide certain material, somewhere like this would have been perfect. But that would have to wait. For the moment, I had enough to go on.

I left the club and made my way outside, thinking about the young man who'd discovered the truth about his mother's death and his own heritage. Charlie had found evidence of various crimes and that he was entitled to money that had been stolen from him. But that knowledge had made him a target for people who'd killed before and wouldn't hesitate to kill again.

The afternoon sun was warm on my face as I walked back to my office, but I felt cold inside. The conspiracy was bigger than I'd imagined, involving not just the Latimers but a network of corrupt officials, union leaders, and businessmen who'd profited from wartime chaos. And at the center of it all was Mick Tierney, the man who'd kept records of everything and used them to maintain his position of power. But Tierney had made one mistake. He'd underestimated Charlie Bristow's determination to learn the truth about his mother. And now that truth was about to destroy the carefully constructed lies that had protected the guilty for seventeen years.

I just hoped I could find Charlie before the people who'd killed his mother decided that the only way to keep their secrets was to silence him forever.

~ Chapter 7 ~

The Latimer mansion looked different in the late afternoon light, its sandstone walls catching the golden glow of the setting sun like old honey. The gardens were immaculate as always, but there was something oppressive about their perfection, as if nature itself had been bullied into submission by the family's will.

I'd come back to Potts Point with more questions than I'd started with, and a growing certainty that the answers lay within the house's elegant walls. Kerrigan's revelations about the charity fund and wartime profiteering had given me the outline of the conspiracy, but I needed details. I needed names, dates, and connections that would tie Charlie's disappearance to the secrets his family had been hiding for seventeen years.

The housemaid who answered the door was the same nervous girl who'd been present when Dominic had shown me to Charlie's room days earlier. She recognized me and stepped back with the kind of wariness that suggested she'd been told to expect my return.

"Mr. Collins," she said, wringing her hands. "I'm not sure —"

"I'm not here to see Mr. Dominic," I said, keeping my voice gentle. "I was hoping to speak with Mrs. Latimer. Mrs. Clara Latimer."

The girl's eyes widened. "Oh sir, I don't think that's a good idea. The mistress isn't well, and Mr. Dominic said—"

"What Mr. Dominic doesn't know won't hurt him." I pressed a pound note into her hand. "Just five minutes. I promise I won't upset her."

The girl looked at the money, then at my face, trying to decide whether a pound was worth the risk of Dominic's anger. Finally, she nodded and stepped aside.

"She's in the conservatory," she whispered. "But please, sir, be quick about it."

The conservatory was at the back of the house, a glass-walled room that looked out over the harbour. It was filled with exotic plants and the kind of expensive furniture that was meant to be looked at rather than used. The air was thick with the scent of orchids and something else—a sweet, medicinal smell that I recognized from my less respectable years.

Clara Latimer was sitting in a wicker chair near the windows, staring out at the water with the kind of vacant expression that came from too much laudanum and too little hope. She was a beautiful woman, or had been once, with dark hair that was streaked with premature gray and skin that had the translucent quality of fine porcelain. But there was something broken about her, something that suggested she'd been fighting a losing battle for years.

"Mrs. Latimer?" I approached carefully, the way you might approach a wounded animal. "I'm George Collins. I'm looking for Charlie Bristow."

She turned to look at me, and for a moment her eyes were sharp and focused. "Charlie," she said, and there was something in her voice that might have been grief. "Poor Charlie."

"You know where he is?"

"I know where he isn't." She laughed, but there was no humor in it. "He isn't safe. He isn't happy. He isn't anywhere he wants to be."

I pulled up a chair and sat down beside her. The harbour was spread out below us, the water catching the last light of the day like scattered diamonds. In the distance, I could see the ferries making their way between the wharves, carrying their cargo of workers and dreamers back to homes they might never own.

"Mrs. Latimer," I said, "I think Charlie discovered something about his family. Something that frightened people who'd rather keep it buried."

She looked at me with eyes that seemed to see through to something beyond the present moment. "Charlie discovered the truth," she said. "And the truth is a dangerous thing in this family."

"What truth?"

"That nothing is what it seems. That the people who raised him aren't who they claim to be. That the money that bought this house and these gardens came from places that decent people don't talk about."

I leaned forward. "Tell me about the chain, Mrs. Latimer. The one Charlie took when he left."

"The chain." She closed her eyes, and when she opened them again, they were clearer than they'd been before. "It belonged to his mother. His real mother."

"Margaret Bristow."

"Margaret." The name came out like a prayer. "She was so young, so beautiful. And so foolish."

"She worked here."

"She worked here. She lived here. She loved here." Clara's voice was getting stronger, as if talking about the past was bringing her back to herself. "She was just a girl from the country, a good family that had hit hard times. She came to the city looking for work. Dominic was in his early-twenties, but he already had his father's appetites."

The pieces were starting to fit together. "Charlie is Dominic's son."

"Charlie is Dominic's son. And Dominic is..." She paused, looking toward the door as if afraid someone might be listening. "Dominic is not the man people think he is."

I waited, sensing that she was working up to something important. The conservatory was growing darker as the sun set, and the plants around us seemed to lean in like an audience waiting for the climax of a play.

"When Charlie's mother became pregnant, there was talk of sending her away," Clara continued. "The family couldn't afford a scandal, especially not with the war starting and business opportunities opening up. But she was stubborn. She said she wouldn't disappear quietly. She said she had rights."

"What happened?"

"Dominic's father made arrangements. She would have the baby, and the family would arrange an adoption. She would be allowed to stay living here, in touch with the child. Everyone would be happy."

"But everyone wasn't happy."

"She wanted Charlie to know the truth. She wanted him to know his true heritage, right or wrong." Clara's hands were trembling now, and she pressed them together in her lap. "She started asking questions about the family's business, about where the money came from. She said she wanted her son to be brought up in a family that was untainted."

"And that's when she became a problem."

"Margaret?" Clara asked, as if that hadn't been who had been talking about all this time. I wondered at that.

"Yes, Margaret. Charlie's mother."

Clara's face drooped in an odd way, a mix of a sorrowful smile and a drug-hazed dream.

"Margaret knew all about this family's hidden sins. She threatened exposure. Wanted money."

This, again, sounded like blackmail. I thought about the letters I'd found in Charlie's room, about Margaret's references to hidden money and dangerous secrets.

"She threatened exposure," Clara repeated. "And when threats didn't work, she tried blackmail." Clara's voice was barely above a whisper. "She had evidence, you see. Documents, photographs, records that she'd copied when she was still trusted. She said she'd hidden them where the family couldn't find them, and that if anything happened to her, other people would know where to look."

"But something did happen to her."

"She died of influenza in 1918. Very sudden, very convenient. The family was properly sorrowful, of course. They gave her a nice funeral and set up a small trust fund for Charlie's education. Everyone said they were being very generous."

"But it wasn't influenza."

Clara looked at me for a long moment, as if deciding whether to trust me with the truth. "I was here the night she died," she said finally. "I was young then, newly married to Dominic, still trying to be the kind of wife he wanted. I heard voices in the library, Margaret's voice and Dominic's. They were arguing about money, about many things I couldn't understand."

"What happened?"

"I don't know exactly. But I heard Margaret scream, and then there was silence. When I went to the library, she was on the floor, and Dominic was standing over her with his hands shaking. He said she'd collapsed, that we needed to call a doctor. But when the doctor came, he said she was already dead."

The conservatory was dark now, lit only by the lights from the harbour and the moon that was rising over the water. Clara's face was pale in the dim light, but her eyes were more alert than they'd been when I'd arrived.

"The doctor was Dr. Pemberton," she continued. "He'd been the family physician for years, and he owed them money. A lot of money. He signed the death certificate without asking too many questions."

"And Charlie never knew."

"He was just a baby, barely walking. The family told him his mother had died of influenza, that she'd been a good woman who'd loved him very much. Isobel showed him the chain a few days ago, said it had belonged to his mother."

"But Charlie started asking more questions."

"Yes. He found Margaret's letters, the ones she'd hidden in his room. He found documents that mentioned the charity fund and his mother's name. He started putting pieces together, and he realized that the story he'd been told wasn't the truth."

I thought about the confrontation in the boarding house, about Tierney's men warning Charlie to give back the chain, warning me off the case. "What made the chain so important?"

"The chain wasn't just jewelry. It was a key." Clara's voice was steady now, as if the act of telling the truth was giving her strength. "Margaret had hidden evidence of the family's wartime activities, and the chain was the key to finding it. She'd told Charlie in her letters that when he was old enough, he should follow the chain to find what rightfully belonged to him."

"And Charlie followed the chain."

"Charlie followed the chain, and he found what Margaret had hidden. Financial records, correspondence, photographs that showed the family's involvement in smuggling and profiteering. Evidence that could destroy them all."

The pieces were falling into place, but there was still something missing. "Where is Charlie now, Mrs. Latimer?"

Clara looked at me with eyes that held a lifetime of regret. "Charlie came to see Dominic on Tuesday afternoon. He had the evidence, and he wanted answers. Not money, not blackmail. Just the truth about his mother and what happened to her."

"What did Dominic say?"

"Dominic said he'd think about it. He told Charlie he would let him know of his decision, that they'd work something out. But after Charlie left, Dominic made phone calls. He called some people, people I don't know. People who solve problems quietly."

A chill ran down my spine. "Has Charlie been back since then?"

"No one has seen Charlie since that afternoon that I can be sure of." Clara's voice was barely audible. "And I'm afraid...I'm afraid that means Dominic has solved his problem the same way he always did."

I thought about the men who'd jumped me in the alley, about their warning to stay away from Tierney. "Why are you telling me this?"

"Because I'm tired of being afraid. Because I'm tired of living with what I know. Because Charlie deserved better than to disappear for the sins of his father." She looked at me with eyes that were fully focused now, as if the laudanum had been burned away by the heat of her confession. "And because someone needs to know the truth before it's too late."

The conservatory was silent except for the sound of water lapping against the harbour walls and the distant noise of the city going about its business. Clara Latimer sat in her wicker chair, looking out at the lights reflected in the water, and I knew that she'd just given me the key to understanding what had happened to Charlie Bristow.

"Mrs. Latimer," I said, "you can't stay here. If Dominic finds out you've talked to me—"

"He already knows." She smiled, and there was something peaceful in her expression. "He's been watching me for days, waiting to see if I'd break. He knows I can't live with the secret anymore."

"Then come with me. I can protect you."

"No one can protect me from Dominic. But I can protect other people from him." She reached into her purse and pulled out a folded piece of paper. "This is everything I know about Margaret's death. Names, dates, places. Everything that Charlie found, and everything that I've known for seventeen years."

I took the paper, feeling the weight of what she was giving me. "This could destroy the family."

"The family destroyed itself long ago. I'm just making sure the truth doesn't die with the people who knew it." She stood up, moving with the careful dignity of someone who'd made a final decision. "But there's more, Mr. Collins. More right here in this house..." Her voice trailed off, whether it was due to fear or the drugs in her system, I couldn't say. Finally, she spoke one last time. "Find Charlie, Mr. Collins. And when you do, make sure people know he was a good boy. Make sure they know he was just trying to find the truth about his mother."

I watched her go, knowing that I'd probably never see her alive again. Clara Latimer had chosen to break the silence that had protected her family for seventeen years, and she'd chosen to pay the price for that decision.

But she'd also given me the weapons I needed to find Charlie Bristow and potentially bring justice to the people who'd killed his mother. The confession in my pocket was more than just evidence—it was a declaration of war against a family that had gotten away with murder for too long. And there was the hint of more. Much more.

I left the conservatory and walked back through the elegant rooms of the Latimer mansion, knowing that I was looking at the fruits of blood money and corruption. The paintings on the walls, the Persian rugs on the floors, the crystal chandeliers that caught the light like captured stars— all of it had been bought with the profits from wartime suffering and the silence of the dead.

But the silence was breaking now, and the truth was finally seeing the light. Charlie Bristow had followed his mother's chain to uncover the family's secrets, and though he'd disappeared, his search for justice wouldn't end with him.

The harbour wind was picking up as I walked back to my car, carrying the smell of salt and secrets that had been buried too long. Charlie Bristow had followed his mother's chain to the truth, and now it was up to me to follow that same chain to find him—before the people who'd killed his mother decided that silence was the only solution to their problems.

Some chains were meant to be broken. And some truths were worth fighting for.

~ Chapter 8 ~

Clara's revelations had given me the key to understanding the Latimer family's secrets, but they had also painted a target on my back. As I headed away from the mansion, I could feel the weight of her words settling over me like a shroud. Margaret Bristow had been murdered for what she knew, and her son Charlie had disappeared after discovering the same dangerous truths. The chain wasn't just jewelry—it was the key to evidence that could destroy the family's carefully constructed facade.

But knowing the truth and proving it were different things entirely. Clara's word alone wouldn't be enough to bring down the Latimers or find Charlie. Enough to cause a scandal, but scandals die down eventually. I needed hard evidence, documents that would stand up in court and convince Tom Majors that the case was worth pursuing despite the political risks.

That evidence, according to Clara, was hidden somewhere in the Latimer mansion. Margaret had secreted away financial records, correspondence, and photographs that documented the family's wartime profiteering and their connections to the charity fund. The chain was the key to finding that evidence, but the chain was gone—clearly taken by whoever had made Charlie disappear.

Unless Clara had been more specific about the situation than I'd realised.

I arrived back at my office and read through Clara's written material, looking for clues I might have missed. She'd mentioned that Margaret had been clever, that she'd hidden things where the family couldn't find them even if they searched. But she'd also said that the chain was necessary to locate the evidence, which suggested that the hiding place itself might be locked or secured in some way.

Then I remembered what Clara had told me near the end: 'There's more, more right here in this house.' Where in the house would someone like Margaret likely hide something where nobody would ever find it? They'd search everywhere for it, every likely place she had easy access to. Then it hit me.

The study. The old man—now Dominic's—private sanctuary, the place where he'd conducted his business and kept his most sensitive documents. If Margaret had found evidence of the family's activities, she might have hidden her own evidence in the same room where the originals were kept, where no one would likely ever even try and look for it. That may have proven true then, but in the ensuing years, even in such an unlikely location, anything hidden there would surely have been found by now.

I waited until well after midnight before returning to Potts Point. The Latimer mansion was dark except for a few security lights, and the streets were empty of everything but cats and the occasional late-night wanderer. I'd learned during my less respectable years that the best time to conduct unofficial business was in the hours between midnight and dawn, when honest people were asleep and the dishonest were too drunk to be observant.

The house's security was more show than substance. The locks were solid but not insurmountable, and the grounds were large enough that a careful man could move through them without attracting attention. I'd brought my tools and a small flashlight, along with a knife that had served me well in similar situations.

I made my way to the rear of the house, where the servants' entrance would provide the most discrete access. The door was locked, but it was an old lock that yielded to pressure applied in the right places. Within minutes, I was inside the house, moving through the dark corridors with the careful steps of someone who knew that discovery would mean more than just embarrassment.

The study was on the ground floor, near the library where Margaret had died. It was a masculine room, all dark wood and leather, with the kind of furniture that suggested serious business conducted by serious men. The walls were lined with books that looked more decorative than functional, and there was a large desk that dominated the center of the room like an altar to commerce.

But it was the safe that interested me most. It was built into the wall behind a painting of some long-dead Latimer ancestor, a heavy steel box that would require more than luck to open. I'd learned safecracking during my time in the army, when military intelligence had required skills that weren't taught in normal schools, and had used those skills successfully in my days of larceny.

The safe was old but well-maintained, the kind of German engineering that was built to last centuries. I worked on it with the patient persistence that the job required, listening for the subtle clicks and feeling for the minute vibrations that would tell me when the tumblers were aligned. It was delicate work, requiring the kind of concentration that made everything else fade into the background.

After what felt like hours but was probably only minutes, the safe clicked open with a satisfaction that was almost musical. Inside were documents that told the story Clara had hinted at. Financial records, correspondence, and photographs that documented the Latimer family's wartime activities. But there was something else, something that made my blood run cold despite the study's stale air.

A letter, written in Margaret Bristow's careful script, addressed to her son Charlie. It was dated just days before her death, and it contained not just evidence of the family's crimes, but also a birth certificate that proved Charlie was Dominic's son. I barely glanced at the rest of the document, knowing I needed to catalogue the rest of the material as quickly as possible.

I read the letter in a hurry, my flashlight beam dancing across the careful handwriting. Margaret had known she was in danger, had known that her questions about the family's wartime activities had made her a target. She'd written to Charlie about the evidence she'd hidden, about the truth of his parentage, about the chain that would lead him to justice when he was old enough to understand.

But there was more. Hidden in her careful script, between the lines of a mother's desperate warning to her son, were further clues that pointed toward evidence she'd hidden in places the family would never think to look. One line stood out: 'The old foundations run deeper than anyone knows, and the men who built them keep their secrets in the dark places below.'

I was memorizing the letter's contents, burning every word into my memory, when I heard it—the soft sound of a footstep in the corridor outside. I froze, my hand still holding the letter, listening to the careful approach of someone who knew the house well.

The footsteps stopped outside the study door. I could hear breathing, slow and deliberate, and then the door opened without a sound.

A figure stepped into the room, moving with practiced silence. I couldn't see who it was—just a shadow against the darkness, but I caught the glint of something metallic in their hand. A knife, thin and sharp, the kind that would slide between ribs without much resistance.

I had no time to think, only to react. I shoved the letter back into the safe and threw myself sideways as the blade came down. The knife caught me in the shoulder, sliding between muscle and bone with a pain that was sharp and immediate.

I rolled away, trying to get to my feet, but my attacker was already moving, pursuing me across the study floor. I couldn't see their face, couldn't tell if it was a man or woman —just a figure in dark clothing moving with lethal intent.

I crashed into the desk, sending papers flying, and managed to get my blackjack out. But the wound in my shoulder was making my left arm useless, and I could feel warm blood soaking through my shirt.

My attacker came at me again, and this time I was ready. I caught their wrist as the knife descended, and for a moment we struggled in the darkness. I heard a sharp intake of breath —whether from pain or exertion, I couldn't tell—and then suddenly they were pulling away, moving toward the door.

I tried to follow, but my legs weren't working properly. The blood loss was making me dizzy, and by the time I reached the corridor, my attacker was gone. I stood there swaying, one hand pressed to my shoulder, listening to the sound of footsteps disappearing into the depths of the house.

I stumbled back to the safe, but I knew I couldn't take the letter. Not now. If it disappeared, the family would know someone had been here. But the contents were burned into my memory—every word, every clue, every piece of evidence that Margaret Bristow had died to protect. But that birth certificate somehow bothered me. There was something about it that I hadn't properly noticed, allowing Dominic's name and my eagerness to peruse everything else override my good sense. It was too late now.

I closed the safe and made my way toward the servants' entrance, my left arm hanging useless at my side. The wound was bleeding freely now, and I had to lean against the wall to keep from falling. Each step was an effort, each breath a reminder that someone wanted me dead.

The harbour wind was cold against my face when I finally reached the street, carrying the smell of salt and secrets that would never see the light of day. I made it to my car and sat behind the wheel for a long moment, trying to stop the bleeding with my handkerchief.

The letter was still in the safe, but its contents were with me. Margaret Bristow had hidden evidence in more places than just the house, and she'd left clues that would lead to that evidence. The line about foundations and dark places below—it meant something specific, something that connected to the charity fund and the wartime activities.

I started the engine and drove slowly back into the city, one hand on the wheel, the other pressed to my shoulder. The pain was constant now, a throbbing reminder of how close I'd come to joining Margaret and Charlie in whatever fate had claimed them.

I cursed what I had failed to properly notice but I also had what I needed for the present. The letter's contents, the clues that would lead me to the evidence Margaret had hidden. The chain of lies was breaking, but the chain of violence was just beginning.

And somewhere in the darkness of Sydney's night, my attacker was reporting back to whoever had sent them, telling them that George Collins was getting too close to the truth for anyone's comfort.

The game was becoming more dangerous, and the stakes were higher than I'd imagined. But I wasn't finished. Not yet.

~ Chapter 9 ~

The doctor at Sydney Hospital had stitched up my shoulder with the kind of professional disinterest that suggested he'd seen worse wounds and asked fewer questions. The morphine they'd given me for the pain had worn off by morning, leaving me with a dull ache that reminded me with every movement that someone wanted me dead.

But pain was a luxury I couldn't afford. Charlie Bristow was still missing, possibly dead, and the letter and the other material I'd found in the safe had given me pieces of the puzzle that were starting to form a picture I didn't like. Margaret Bristow had been murdered for what she knew, and her son had disappeared after discovering the same dangerous truths. And the diamond chain, the valueless piece of jewelry, was still nowhere to be found.

I needed to find Mick Tierney. Clara had mentioned him in her confession, and Big Sid at the union hall had confirmed that Charlie had been asking questions about the man. If Tierney was involved in Charlie's disappearance, then he was the thread I needed to pull to unravel the whole thing.

Big Sid had told me at our last meeting where Tierney was likely to be found, but I wanted another word with the man beforehand. I found him at his usual table in the union hall, nursing a beer and reading yesterday's newspaper with the kind of concentration that suggested he was avoiding something.

"Mick's been asking questions about you," he said without looking up from the paper. "Word is he's not happy about your interest in the Bristow boy."

"I can find him at that Darling Harbour warehouse?"

"If you're stupid enough to go looking for him, yeah. He's been using it for business meetings lately."

"What kind of business?"

"The kind that's conducted after dark and paid for in cash." Sid finished his beer and stood up. "Collins, you've got a reputation for being clever. Don't ruin it by getting yourself killed over something that's already finished."

But Charlie Bristow wasn't finished. He was still missing, still potentially in danger, and the material I'd found in the Latimer safe had made it clear that he was more than just an adopted child looking for answers. He was Dominic's biological child, and that made him a threat to more than just the family's reputation.

I spent the rest of the day preparing for what I knew would be a dangerous meeting. I cleaned my pistol, checked my knife, and made sure my shoulder wound wouldn't slow me down when quick movement meant the difference between breathing and bleeding. Then I wrote a letter to Tom Majors, explaining what I'd learned and where I was going, and left it in my office safe. Insurance, in case I didn't come back to collect it.

The warehouse in question was a relic from Sydney's shipping boom, a massive brick building that squatted on the harbour like a sleeping giant. Most of the windows were broken, and the loading docks were empty except for the rats that had made the place their kingdom. But there was light coming from the second floor, and I could hear voices carrying across the water.

I made my way around to the back of the building, where a fire escape provided access to the upper floors. The metal stairs were rusty and treacherous, but they held my weight as I climbed toward the light.

The window I chose was cracked but not broken, and it gave me a clear view of the building's interior. The space had been converted into a makeshift office, with crates serving as furniture and electric lights strung from the ceiling beams. Two men were sitting at a table made from a shipping crate, playing cards and drinking from a bottle of whiskey.

From the way he was described to me, one of them was Mick Tierney.

He was smaller than I'd expected, a wiry man with prematurely gray hair and the kind of face that suggested he'd been in too many fights and won just enough of them to stay alive. His hands were scarred, and he moved with the careful economy of someone who knew that wasted motion could be fatal.

The other man was younger, broader, with the thick neck and cauliflower ears of a boxer who'd taken too many hits to the head. He was losing at cards, and his frustration was making him careless with his money and his mouth.

I waited until the boxer had drunk enough whiskey to make his reactions slow, then I made my move. The window opened with a squeal of protest, and I climbed through into the warehouse.

"Good evening, gentlemen," I said, my pistol in my hand but not yet pointed at anyone. "I was hoping we could have a conversation."

Tierney looked up from his cards with the kind of calm that suggested he'd been expecting me. "George 'Magpie' Collins. I was wondering when you'd show up."

The boxer reached for something under the table, but Tierney stopped him with a gesture. "Easy, Jimmy. Mr. Collins is here to talk, not to fight. Isn't that right, Collins?"

"That depends on what you have to say about Charlie Bristow."

Tierney set down his cards and leaned back in his chair. "Charlie Bristow. Poor bastard. I didn't hurt him, though, I swear. Not him. But he got himself mixed up in something that was way over his head."

"What kind of something?"

"The kind that gets people killed." Tierney poured himself another whiskey and gestured for me to sit down. "But I suppose you already know that, considering someone tried to carve you up last night."

"You'd know all about that," I said sharply.

"What are you talking about?"

"You sent your boys after me recently."

"I don't know what you're talking about, mate. I sent nobody after you, and I mean that. Now sit."

I don't know why, but I believed him. I kept my pistol ready but accepted the invitation to sit. "Tell me about Charlie then."

Tierney studied my face for a moment, as if deciding how much truth I could handle. "Charlie came to me about a week ago. He had questions about his family, about his mother, about things that happened during the war. He thought I might have answers."

"Did you?"

"I had some answers. Not all of them, but enough to make him understand how much trouble he was in." Tierney took a sip of his whiskey. "Charlie wasn't just some adopted kid looking for his roots. He was Dominic Latimer's son, and he'd found evidence that could destroy the family."

"Evidence about the charity fund."

"Evidence about a lot of things. Wartime profiteering, smuggling, bribery, murder. The Latimers had been busy during the war, and Charlie had found the receipts." Tierney's voice was matter-of-fact, as if he were discussing the weather. "He wanted to know what to do with what he'd found."

"What did you tell him?"

"I told him to forget about it. He had it good, to just go home and live off his trust fund." Tierney met my eyes. "But Charlie was young and idealistic. He thought justice was more important than survival."

I thought about the letter I'd found in the safe, about Margaret Bristow's desperate attempt to protect her son from the truth. "What was your connection to the family?"

"I worked for them during the war. Security, mostly. Making sure cargo got from point A to point B without attracting the wrong kind of attention." Tierney's smile was bitter. "I was good at my job, and they paid well. But I wasn't family, so when the war ended, they didn't need me anymore."

"But you stayed connected."

"I stayed interested. The Latimers had made a lot of money during the war, and some of it had come from places that decent people didn't like to think about. I kept records, insurance policies in case they ever decided I knew too much."

The pieces were starting to fit together. "And Charlie found those records."

"Charlie found some of them, some others as well. But more importantly, he found his mother's evidence. And then Margaret Bristow had been smarter than anyone gave her credit for. She'd documented everything, photographed everything, saved everything. And she'd hidden it all where the family couldn't find it."

Mother? And then Margaret Bristow? Something wasn't adding up.

"The chain was the key."

"The chain was the key. Margaret had hidden her evidence in a safety deposit box, and the chain was the key to finding it. Not literally, but close enough." Tierney finished his whiskey and poured another. "Charlie had the chain, and he had his mother's instructions. He knew where to look."

"So what happened?"

"Charlie found the evidence. All of it. Financial records, correspondence, photographs that showed the family's involvement in activities that would have made them very unpopular if they'd become public." Tierney's voice was getting harder. "But Charlie made a mistake. He trusted the wrong person."

"Who?"

"Someone who was supposed to help him. Someone who was supposed to be on his side." Tierney looked at me with eyes that held years of accumulated cynicism. "Charlie thought he'd found an ally. Instead, he'd found his enemy."

The warehouse was quiet except for the sound of water lapping against the dock pilings and the distant noise of the city going about its business. Jimmy the boxer had passed out in his chair, and his snoring provided a grotesque counterpoint to our conversation.

"Why are you telling me all this?"

Tierney's expression changed, becoming softer and more complicated. "Isobel. My Isobel. Beautiful, intelligent, trapped in a family that treated her like a piece of property." He paused, choosing his words carefully. "We were...close. Had been for several months. But then–"

"Close enough to plan an escape?" I interrupted.

"Close enough to dream about one. The chain was supposed to be our ticket out. Charlie had found it, had used it to locate his mother's evidence, but he was willing to share what he'd found. He wanted justice, but he also wanted his family to be safe." Tierney's voice was bitter. "He was protecting people who were planning to betray him."

"What was the plan?"

"Simple. Charlie would use the evidence to force the family to acknowledge him as Dominic's son. Not publicly, but privately. He wanted his inheritance, his rightful place, his name cleared. In exchange, he'd keep quiet about the wartime activities." Tierney stared into his whiskey. "And Isobel and I would take enough money to disappear. Start over somewhere the Latimer name didn't carry weight."

"But it went wrong."

"It went wrong because Charlie underestimated how far his family was willing to go to protect their secrets." Tierney looked up at me. "And because I underestimated how much Isobel loved her family."

The temperature in the warehouse seemed to drop. "What do you mean?"

"I mean that when Charlie confronted Dominic with the evidence, Isobel was there. She heard everything. She saw the photographs, the documents, the proof of what her family had done during the war." Tierney's hands were shaking now. "And she chose her family over justice. Over Charlie. Over me."

"She told Dominic about your plan."

"She told Dominic everything. About our relationship, about the escape plan, about Charlie's plans." Tierney's voice was flat. "She betrayed everyone who'd trusted her."

"Where is Charlie now?"

"I don't know. After the meeting went wrong, Charlie disappeared. That was a few days ago, Tuesday I think." Tierney's voice was strained. "I've been looking for him too, but I think we might be too late."

"What makes you say that?"

"Because Dominic doesn't leave loose ends. And Charlie became a very dangerous loose end the moment he walked into that meeting." Tierney stood up, swaying slightly from the whiskey. "Charlie's out there somewhere, and he's either hiding or he's..."

"Or he's what?"

"Or he's beyond help." Tierney moved toward the window, looking out at the harbour. "Either way, asking questions about him is going to get us both killed."

"I need to find him."

"You need to stay alive." Tierney turned back to me. "Charlie made his choice when he decided to trust his family. Now he has to live with the consequences."

"And you?"

"I have to live with being a fool. But at least I'll be a living fool." Tierney walked back to the table and picked up his cards. "You should go now, Collins. Before someone decides you know too much."

I stood up, keeping my pistol ready. "This isn't over."

"It is for me. And if you're smart, it'll be over for you too." Tierney didn't look up from his cards. "But I know you're not smart. You're stubborn, and stubborn people don't live long in this business."

I made my way back to the window, climbed out onto the fire escape, and descended into the Sydney night. The harbour wind was sharp and cold, carrying the smell of salt and secrets that would never see the light of day.

Charlie Bristow was still missing, and the evidence Margaret Bristow had died to protect was in the hands of people who would kill to keep it hidden. But I wasn't finished. Charlie might be in danger, but justice didn't have to die with him. And somewhere in the elegant halls of the Latimer mansion, there were still secrets waiting to be uncovered, still lies waiting to be exposed. And I had a horrible feeling there was a truth I was only just starting to come to terms with.

The chain of violence was continuing, but it was also creating new links. And sometimes, if you were patient enough and stubborn enough, you could use those links to bind the people who thought they were untouchable.

The game was far from over.

~ Chapter 10 ~

Margaret Bristow's letter had been more than a confession—it had been a map. Though I'd been forced to leave it behind in the safe, bleeding from my attacker's knife, I'd burned every word into my memory during those precious minutes I'd had to read it.

I sat in my office the next evening, my shoulder still throbbing from the wound, reconstructing the letter's contents in my mind. Margaret had been clever, perhaps cleverer than anyone had given her credit for. She knew exactly where the Latimer family had kept all their dirty laundry, in a place that would have been impossible for a simple housemaid to access.

The clue was in a single line I'd memorized, almost throwaway in its casualness: "The old foundations run deeper than anyone knows, and the men who built them keep their secrets in the dark places below."

The NSW Masonic Club. The place where I'd first heard about the charity fund, where Abe Kerrigan had told me about the Latimer patriarch's connections to the wartime smuggling operations. But Margaret's cryptic words suggested there was more to the club than its public face—something hidden beneath the respectable veneer of brotherhood and business.

I waited until the following evening before making my move. The club would be busy with its dinner service, the members occupied with their port and their politics. It was the kind of distraction that would give me the cover I needed to explore the parts of the building that weren't meant for casual visitors.

The club's main entrance was too visible, too well-monitored. But buildings like this always had service entrances, delivery doors, and maintenance access that were less carefully watched. I found what I was looking for in the alley behind the building: a heavy wooden door marked "Staff Only" that opened onto a narrow corridor leading to the club's kitchen.

The lock was solid but not insurmountable. I'd learned during my less respectable years that the best way to open locked doors was to understand the minds of the people who'd locked them. This was a service entrance, meant to keep out casual intruders but not to stop someone with the right tools and the patience to use them.

The corridor beyond was lit by a single electric bulb that cast harsh shadows across the brick walls. I could hear the sounds of the kitchen—the clatter of dishes, the murmur of conversation, the occasional bark of orders from the head cook. The dinner service was in full swing, which meant the staff would be too busy to notice one more figure moving through the building's less public spaces.

I made my way through the corridors, following the building's logic toward its foundations. The club had been formed in 1893, the current clubhouse completed in 1927, and it had the kind of solid construction that suggested it was meant to last centuries. But it also had the kind of hidden spaces that Georgian architects had loved—basement storage rooms, wine cellars, and maintenance areas that honeycombed the building's lower levels.

The staircase I found was narrow and steep, leading down into darkness that seemed to swallow the light from my electric torch. The air grew colder as I descended, carrying the smell of old stone and secrets that had been buried too long.

The basement was larger than I'd expected, a series of connected rooms that stretched beneath the entire building. Some were clearly meant for storage—wine racks, filing cabinets, boxes of supplies that spoke of the club's daily operations. But others were different, older, with the kind of furnishings that suggested they'd once been meeting rooms.

It was in the third room that I found what I was looking for.

The space had been converted into a storage area, but the conversion had been hasty and incomplete. Behind a stack of chairs and tables, I found what had once been a proper meeting room, complete with ceremonial furnishings and symbols that spoke of the club's more secretive functions.

But it was the vault that caught my attention. Built into the wall behind a heavy steel door, it was the kind of secure storage that suggested the club's wartime activities had been more extensive than anyone wanted to admit. The door was locked, but the mechanism was old and the lock was one I'd encountered before during my military service.

Inside the vault were documents that told a story darker than even Clara's confession had suggested. Financial records, correspondence, and photographs that documented not just the Latimer family's wartime profiteering, but the entire network of corruption that had flourished during the war years.

And there, in a leather satchel that matched the one Mrs Kowalski had mentioned, was the rest of the evidence Margaret Bristow had died to protect.

The satchel contained everything. Photographs of smuggling operations, financial records showing payments to government officials, correspondence between the Latimer patriarch and German agents. But there was something else, something that made my blood run cold despite the vault's stale air.

A bloodstained handkerchief, monogrammed with the initials "C.B." The stains were fresh, no more than a few days old, and they told a story that I didn't want to believe.

But there was more. Bundled with the handkerchief was a collection of union documents that implicated not just the Latimers, but half the city's political establishment in a web of corruption that stretched from the waterfront to the halls of government. Dominic Latimer's name appeared on dozens of documents, always in connection with payments, bribes, and favors that had allowed the family's wartime activities to flourish.

The union documents were the final piece of the puzzle. They showed how the charity fund had been used to launder money from the smuggling operations, how union officials had been bought to ensure labor peace, how government inspectors had been paid to look the other way. It was a system of corruption so complete that it had infected every level of Sydney's power structure.

But the bloodstained handkerchief was what worried me most. It was proof that Charlie had been here, in this room, and that he'd been hurt. The question was whether he'd left under his own power or whether someone had carried him out. Either way, no one thought anyone else would ever find this evidence.

I photographed everything I could, using the small camera I'd brought for just this purpose. The documents were too bulky to steal, but the photographs would provide the evidence I needed to build a case that even Tom Majors couldn't ignore.

As I worked, I became aware of sounds from above—footsteps in the corridor, voices that seemed to be moving in my direction. The dinner service was winding down, and the staff would be cleaning up, securing the building for the night. If I was discovered here, in the club's most secret room, there would be no explanation that would keep me breathing.

I gathered the documents quickly, replacing them in the vault exactly as I'd found them. The satchel and handkerchief I left untouched—they were evidence, but taking them would alert whoever had put them there that the vault had been compromised.

The footsteps were getting closer. I could hear voices now, low and urgent, discussing something that made them sound worried. I closed the vault, arranged the furniture to hide the entrance, and made my way toward the staircase.

The corridor above was empty, but I could hear movement in the distance. I made my way back toward the service entrance, moving quickly but quietly through the building's maze of corridors. The kitchen was still busy, the staff occupied with the cleanup from the dinner service.

I slipped out through the service entrance and into the alley, where the night air felt clean and cold after the stale atmosphere of the vault. The city was alive around me, but I felt like I was carrying death in my pocket—the photographs that would destroy the Latimer family, and the knowledge that Charlie Bristow had been in that room, bleeding, only days before.

The documents I'd found painted a picture of corruption that went far beyond a single family's greed. They showed a system of bribery and influence that had turned the war into a profit center for men who'd never seen a battlefield. The Latimers had been part of it, but they hadn't been alone.

But it was the bloodstained handkerchief that haunted me as I walked back to my office. Charlie had been in that vault, had found the evidence his mother had died to protect. And then something had happened, something that had left his blood on a piece of cloth and his satchel abandoned in a room that was supposed to be secret.

The chain of evidence was complete now. I had the documents, the photographs, the proof of what the Latimer family had done during the war. But I also had the growing certainty that Charlie Bristow was running out of time.

The question was whether I could find him before whoever had put his bloodstained handkerchief in that vault decided that loose ends needed to be tied off permanently. Or perhaps was already too late for Charlie? I had to know the truth. Charlie deserved that. So did Margaret.

The game was entering its final phase, and the stakes were higher than I'd ever imagined. Justice was within reach, but it would come at a price that might be more than any of us could afford to pay.

~ Chapter 11 ~

The photographs from the vault were spread across my desk like a tarot reading that spelled out corruption and death. Each image told part of the story—wartime profiteering, political payoffs, a network of bribes that had turned the war into a profit center for men who'd never heard a shot fired in anger. But it was the bloodstained handkerchief that haunted me, the proof that Charlie Bristow had been in that room and had left his blood behind.

This was all Tom needed to make an arrrest, the kind of concrete evidence even those above him couldn't ignore. Clara's written confession was no longer needed. I'd call Tom and let him raid the club at his discretion, but I first needed to come to terms with a truth I had begrudgingly realized after talking to Tierney. It was horrendous, but it all made sense now.

I'd been staring at the evidence for hours, thinking about this truth, when I heard footsteps on the stairs outside my office. They were light, careful, the kind of steps that belonged to someone who didn't want to be heard. I slipped the photographs into my desk drawer and put my hand on the service revolver I'd taken to carrying since the knife attack.

The door opened without a knock, and Isobel Latimer stepped into my office like a ghost returning to haunt the living. She was still wearing the dove-grey coat from our first meeting, but now it hung on her frame like a shroud. Her face was pale, her eyes red-rimmed, and she moved with the careful precision of someone who was holding herself together through sheer force of will.

"Mr. Collins," she said, her voice barely above a whisper. "Have you made any progress with the case?"

I gestured to the chair across from my desk, but she remained standing, her hands clasped in front of her like a penitent at confession. The afternoon light from my window cast harsh shadows across her face, making her look older than her years.

"I have," I said, before deciding to lay my bomb on her. "And I know the truth. All of it."

"The truth about what, Mr. Collins?"

"About everything."

She took a shaky breath and practically staggered into the guest chair, pale as a ghost. I leaned back in mine, studying her face. There was something different about her now, a desperation that hadn't been there during our first meeting. The careful composure was cracking, and what showed through the cracks was fear.

"I'm listening."

"Charlie was your son, not your adopted brother."

Tears streaked through her makeup and she nodded ever-so-slightly.

"The chain was yours, not Margaret Bristow's," I continued. "Margaret was just the housemaid, coerced into acting as the boy's real mother. The letters she wrote to him were fake. You wrote them, didn't you?"

The tears flowed more freely now and the nodding became more noticeable with each passing fact.

"But then Margaret got greedy, tried blackmailing the family. So Dominic took care of that. And when Charlie got curious, found out things he shouldn't have, you betrayed him and–"

"No!" Isobel cried, her face writ with grief. She jerked to her feet and began to pace, her movements jerky and uncontrolled. "That's not how it was, at least..."

Her voice trailed away and I wondered if she even knew what to say next. I decided I had to prompt her. "Then why don't you tell me exactly how it was."

She took a deep breath, and I could tell the truth, or at least her truth, was waiting to spill out. "I told you Charlie was my adopted brother. I told you he'd run off with a chain of no great value."

"Yes, you did."

"I lied about all of it." The words came out in a rush, as if she'd been holding them back for days. "You were right, Charlie wasn't my brother. He was my son."

The admission hung in the air between us like smoke from a funeral pyre. I'd already laid this truth on her only seconds ago, but hearing it from Isobel herself was somehow different. It was a confession that carried the weight of years of deception. And there was also that word–was.

"Go on."

She stopped pacing and looked at me directly for the first time since entering my office. "I was fifteen when it happened. Just fifteen. Dominic was twenty-two, handsome, charming. He told me he loved me, that we'd be married someday. I believed him."

"Your own brother?" The horror of it kept bashing away at me.

"Half-brother," she said, as if the distinction mattered. "My father married his mother when Dominic was already grown. We weren't raised together, didn't know each other well. When I came to live in the house..."

She trailed off, lost in memories that were obviously painful. I waited, giving her time to find her words, but the horror of it was almost as painful for me.

"When I found out I was pregnant, I thought he'd do the right thing. But the family couldn't afford a scandal. My father had political ambitions, business interests. Dominic was being groomed to take over the family concerns. A bastard child with his half-sister would have destroyed everything."

"So you gave birth in secret."

"They sent me away. To a private hospital in Melbourne, where they said I'd died in childbirth. The baby—Charlie—was officially orphaned. Then, a few months later, the family adopted him out of 'Christian charity.' The perfect solution."

I thought about the young man I'd seen in the photographs, the earnest face that had reminded me of someone I couldn't quite place. Now I knew why—he'd had his mother's eyes, the same grey-green that was watching me now.

"And the chain?"

Her composure cracked completely. More tears flowed down her cheeks, and she collapsed back into the chair as if her legs could no longer support her. "The chain belonged to my mother. My real mother, who died when I was born. It was the only thing I had left of her."

"You gave it to Charlie."

"Just last week, I told him the truth. About who he really was, about what had happened. I thought he deserved to know. I just couldn't hide the truth from him anymore. And I gave him the chain, the only inheritance I could offer him."

The pieces were falling into place now, forming a picture that was uglier than I'd imagined. Charlie knew Isobel was his mother. "And what about Margaret? The fabricated story of her being Charlie's mother was all for nothing."

"She was Dominic's mistress," Isobel explained. "She agreed to act as Charlie's mother if and when Charlie ever became curious. But, when Dominic's eye began to wander elsewhere, she sought revenge. She knew all the family secrets, realised she could make enough money through blackmail to reestablish herself in a fine position within society."

"So Dominic killed her."

She nodded again.

"And what of Charlie? I imagine he wanted more than just the truth."

"He wanted justice." Her voice was bitter. "After I told him the truth, he realised he had grown up watching Dominic live in luxury while his real mother—me—pretended to be his sister. He'd seen the family's power, their wealth, their influence. And he wanted to know where it had all come from. And he wanted some form of justice for me."

"So he started digging."

"He found out about the wartime activities, the charity fund, the smuggling operations. He found documents, evidence that could have destroyed the family. And he threatened to expose everything unless Dominic acknowledged him as his son, while continuing the charade of Margaret Bristow as his real mother. To preserve my honour."

"And Dominic refused."

"Dominic laughed at him. Called him a bastard, a nobody who should be grateful for the scraps the family had thrown him. He said Charlie would never be anything more than a servant's son–almost as though Margaret actually had been his mother all along–no matter what his blood might be."

The hatred in her voice was like acid, corrosive and deadly. She was talking about her half-brother, but also about the father of her child, the man who'd used her and then discarded her when it became inconvenient.

"That's when you betrayed Charlie."

"I did nothing of the sort," Isobel wailed. "Dominic threatened me, threatened to cast me out, then threatened to kill me. I tried to talk Charlie out of hurting the family, tried to–"

"That's when Dominic killed him."

"He couldn't risk exposure. The family's reputation, their business interests, their political connections—it was all worth more to him than his own son's life." The words came out flat, matter-of-fact, as if she was discussing the weather.

"Where's the chain now?"

"Dominic has it. Claims it's his now, that it always should have been his. It is very valuable."

I suspected as much. Likely Dominic prized it as some sort of demented trophy. I leaned forward, my hands flat on the desk. "Do you have proof of any of this?"

She looked away, her fingers twisting in her lap. "I know my brother. I know what he's capable of. Charlie threatened everything Dominic had built, everything he'd inherited. He would have done anything to protect that."

"But no proof."

"No," she whispered. "No proof. Just the certainty that comes from knowing someone as I know Dominic, from seeing what they'll do to protect themselves."

She stood up, smoothing down her coat with shaking hands. The afternoon light was fading, casting long shadows across my office. Outside, the city was settling into evening, unaware that in this small room, a family's darkest secrets were finally being dragged into the light.

"There's something else," she said. "The chain—it was never just about the inheritance. It was almost as though it was cursed, Mr. Collins. Every woman in my family who'd owned it had died young, died badly. My mother, my grandmother, and now..."

She didn't finish the sentence, but I could see the fear in her eyes. I knew the curse she was referring to was simply that attached to any valuable jewel: the lust of owning such often lead to violence. Whether Isobel actually believed in a real curse, I couldn't say.

She walked to the door, then paused with her hand on the handle. "I hired you ostensibly to find Charlie, Mr. Collins. But I knew he was already dead. I hired you because I knew you'd dig deeper than anyone else would. I knew you'd uncover the truth about what Dominic is capable of. I hoped you could bring him to justice for taking my dear, sweet boy from me. From ruining all our lives." She took another deep breath. "I'm asking you to find proof. Real proof. The kind that will stand up in court, that will make people believe what I know in my heart to be true."

She didn't know I already had enough proof to send her brother to prison for life.

She opened the door, then looked back at me one last time. "Find him, Mr. Collins. Find Charlie and give him the justice he deserves. It's the only thing I can give him now."

Then she was gone, leaving behind only the smell of her perfume and the weight of a confession that had explained everything while proving nothing.

I sat in the gathering darkness, thinking about chains—chains of evidence, chains of corruption, chains of family lies that bound people together in ways that destroyed them all. Somewhere in the harbour, Charlie Bristow was waiting for justice. And Dominic, his killer, was waiting too, thinking he'd covered his tracks well enough to escape.

He was wrong.

I had a call to make, and I had to try and wash the stench of evil from my soul.

~ Chapter 12 ~

The telephone rang at half past six in the morning, cutting through the grey Sydney dawn like a blade. I'd been awake for hours, sitting in my office chair with a cup of coffee that had gone cold, staring at the photographs from the vault and thinking about chains, broken and otherwise.

"Collins." My voice was rough with sleeplessness.

"It's Majors." Tom's voice was tight, professional, the tone he used when he was calling about official business. "You need to get down to Circular Quay. We've got a body."

My heart sunk but I knew in my soul who it was. My thirst for justice was only increasing.

The harbour was wrapped in morning mist, the kind that made the city look like a ghost town populated by shadows. I found Tom standing on the wharf near the ferry terminal, his coat collar turned up against the damp wind that carried the smell of salt and diesel fuel. A small crowd of early commuters and dock workers had gathered at a respectful distance, drawn by the morbid curiosity that always accompanied sudden death.

"Good to see you, Magpie," he greeted me.

"When?" I asked, joining him at the railing.

"Harbour patrol found him about an hour ago. Fisherman spotted something in the water near the Quay, thought it might be driftwood." Tom's face was grim. "It wasn't."

The body was already on the dock, covered by a tarpaulin that did little to hide the shape beneath. The harbour police were keeping the crowd back while the coroner's men went about their business with the methodical efficiency of people who'd seen too much death to be surprised by it anymore.

"You think it's him?"

"I think you'd better take a look."

Tom led me over to where the body lay. The coroner, a thin man with wire-rimmed spectacles and the pale complexion of someone who spent his days with the dead, nodded to us as we approached.

"Morning, Inspector. Mr. Collins." He knew me from previous cases, the kind where official channels weren't quite wide enough for all the truth that needed to flow through them.

"What can you tell us, Doc?"

"Male, approximately nineteen or twenty years old. Been in the water for a few days—I'd estimate four or five, based on the condition of the remains." He pulled back the tarpaulin with the casual professionalism of a man discussing the time of day. "Cause of death appears to be blunt force trauma to the head, followed by drowning."

I looked down at what had once been Charlie Bristow and felt something cold settle in my stomach. The harbour had not been kind to him. His face was swollen and discolored, his dark hair matted with seaweed and debris. But it was unmistakably the young man I'd seen in the photographs, the earnest face that had carried his mother's eyes.

"Any identification?"

"Nothing. Whoever did this was thorough—no wallet, no papers, no jewelry. Just the clothes on his back." The coroner gestured to the sodden garments laid out on a nearby tarpaulin. "Undershirt, trousers, socks. No shoes, no jacket."

"Bound?"

"Wrists and ankles. Rope, probably from a boat. And weighted down with what looks like engine parts—bits of metal that would have kept him on the bottom if the ropes hadn't rotted through."

I studied the body, taking in the details that would matter later. The hands were soft, unmarked by manual labor—the hands of someone who'd been raised in comfort even if he'd never been acknowledged as family. The build was slight but athletic, the kind that came from cricket and tennis rather than dock work.

"Any sign of a struggle?"

"Apart from the head wound, no. But that doesn't mean much—he could have been unconscious when he went into the water."

Tom was writing in his notebook, recording the facts with the careful precision of a man who knew that cases like this could disappear if they weren't documented properly. "Time of death?"

"He was last seen Tuesday night," I cut in.

"Based on the condition of the body and the water temperature," the coroner said, "I'd say he's been dead since Tuesday night then. That would be my best guess at this stage."

The mist was starting to lift, revealing the harbour in all its morning glory. Ferries were beginning their runs, carrying office workers and shopgirls to another day of honest labor. The city was waking up, unaware that one of its sons had been returned to it in the worst possible way.

"Anything else?"

The coroner shook his head. "I'll know more after the post-mortem, but it's a straightforward case of murder. Someone hit him hard enough to crack his skull, then dumped him in the harbour hoping he'd never be found."

I looked down at Charlie's face one more time, memorizing the features that would haunt me until this case was closed. Somewhere in the city, his killer was going about his business, thinking he'd covered his tracks well enough to escape justice. Somewhere else, Isobel Latimer was waiting for news that would either free her from twenty years of lies or condemn her to a lifetime of guilt.

"I need to make a call," I told Tom.

He understood, then closed his notebook and looked out over the harbour, where the morning sun was beginning to burn through the mist. "I intend raiding the Masonic Club later this morning. If the evidence there is as you say it is–"

"It is."

"Then we can make some headway with this case. If not for murder then for so much else."

I understood. The Latimer name carried enough weight to normally sink an investigation before it ever saw the light of day. But not with the evidence that I saw and photographed at the club. No name could make that go away.

"I'll back you up," I said, for what it was worth, knowing full well Tom had a family to think about. "Whatever the cost."

He smiled in understanding. We stood in silence for a moment, watching the harbour police load Charlie's body into the coroner's wagon. The crowd was beginning to disperse, the morning's drama already becoming yesterday's news. In a few hours, the newspapers would run a small item about an unidentified body found in the harbour, and by evening, even that would be forgotten.

"There's something else," Tom said quietly. "The rope that was used to bind him—it's not the kind you'd find on just any boat. It's the kind used on expensive private yachts, the kind that rich men use for weekend sailing."

"The Latimers have a yacht?"

"Half the wealthy families in Sydney have yachts. But yes, they have one. Berth 47 at the Royal Sydney Yacht Squadron."

I memorized the number, another piece of evidence that would either hang a killer or disappear into the bureaucratic maze that protected the powerful from the consequences of their actions.

"I'll be in touch," I told Tom.

"Be careful, mate. Charlie Bristow is dead, but that doesn't mean the killing is over."

I walked back through the city as the morning rush began in earnest. Trams clanged along their tracks, shop girls hurried to their jobs, and businessmen read their newspapers over coffee and cigarettes. It was a normal morning in a normal city, except for the fact that somewhere in its midst, a killer was walking free.

The harbour wind followed me through the streets, carrying the smell of salt and secrets that would never see the light of day. Charlie Bristow had died for what he knew, and now it was up to me to make sure his death counted for something.

The chain of evidence was almost complete. All I needed now was the link that would connect the killer to his crime of murder—and the courage to use it, regardless of the consequences.

The dead sea had given up its secrets. Now it was time to make the living pay for them.

~ Chapter 13 ~

The pieces of the puzzle had been scattered across Sydney like leaves in a harbour wind, but now they were coming together with the inevitable clarity of a noose tightening around a neck. I sat in my office as the afternoon light slanted through the venetian blinds, staring at the evidence laid out on my desk: the various photographs I'd taken from what I had found at the club, while also mulling over all the other information I'd seen and others I'd been told.

Dominic Latimer had killed his own son—not his brother, but his son—to protect a fortune built on wartime profiteering and political corruption. He'd killed Charlie, stole the chain that Isobel had given to the lad, stabbed me and had his hired thugs try to mess me up, using Mick Tierney as a convenient patsy for all that to muddy the waters. But knowing all this and proving it were two different things entirely, and the kind of proof that would stick to a Latimer was harder to come by than honest politicians in Sydney. What I had found would put the bastard away for his myriad other crimes, but not for murder. Justice for Charlie would be fleeting at best. These thoughts and more burned in my mind as I waited to hear from Tom about his raid and potential arrest of the man in question.

The telephone rang, cutting through my thoughts like a blade through silk. It was no doubt Tom.

"Collins."

"It's Clara." The voice was different—clearer, more focused than I'd ever heard it. The laudanum fog had lifted, leaving behind something sharp and dangerous. "I need to see you. Now."

"Mrs. Latimer—"

"The old boatshed at Rushcutters Bay. Do you know it?"

In my line of work, I did. A derelict structure that had been abandoned since the war, the kind of place where Sydney's secrets went to die. "I'll be there in twenty minutes."

"Come alone. And bring your notebook."

The line went dead, leaving me with the sound of my own breathing and the distant hum of the city going about its business. I gulped down my cold coffee, checked the revolver in my shoulder holster, and headed for the door. Whatever Clara Latimer had to say, it was going to be worth hearing.

The boatshed squatted on the water's edge like a dying animal, its weathered boards grey with age and salt spray. The harbour lapped against its pilings with the sound of a clock counting down to midnight. I found Clara standing inside, silhouetted against the opening that faced the water. She was wearing a simple black dress and no jewelry, looking more like a widow than a woman whose husband was still alive.

"Thank you for coming," she said without turning around. "I wasn't sure you would."

"Why here?"

"Because it's the only place in Sydney where Dominic's money can't buy ears." She turned to face me, and I saw that her eyes were clear for the first time since I'd met her. The laudanum had been replaced by something harder—resolve, perhaps, or the kind of desperate courage that came from having nothing left to lose.

"You know, don't you?" she said. "About Charlie. About what Dominic did."

"Isobel told you?"

She nodded grimly.

"Yes, I know he killed him. I know why. What I don't know is how to prove it."

Clara reached into her purse and withdrew a folded piece of paper, heavy stock with the Latimer family crest embossed at the top. "This might help."

I took the paper and unfolded it, revealing several pages of handwriting in a mixture of a man's kempt but also strangely sloppy script. The heading read: "The Full and Complete Confession of Dominic Charles Latimer, written in my own hand this day, April 3, 1935."

"He wrote this?"

"Last night. He was drunk—drunker than I'd seen him in years. He was raving about Charlie, about how the boy had ruined everything, how he'd had no choice." Clara's voice was steady, but her hands were shaking. "He passed out at his desk, and I found him there this morning with the confession beside him. He'd written it all down—every detail, every lie, every moment of that night."

I read quickly, my eyes scanning the handwriting that laid out the whole ugly truth. Dominic had arranged to meet

Charlie at the family yacht the night he disappeared, ostensibly to discuss a financial settlement that would keep the boy quiet about his parentage. But Charlie had refused to be bought off. He wasn't after money. He demanded recognition, legitimacy, his proper place in the family. And when Dominic had refused, Charlie had threatened to go to the newspapers with everything—the birth certificate, the wartime profiteering, the political payoffs that had built the Latimer fortune, the works.

"He hit him with a marlinspike," Clara continued, her voice flat and emotionless. "That's what he wrote. Charlie went down hard, blood everywhere. Dominic thought he was dead, but he was still breathing. So he..." She stopped, unable to continue.

"So he finished the job," I said, filling in the blanks that the confession had laid out in brutal detail. "Tied him up with yacht rope, and dumped him in the harbour."

"The chain was in Charlie's pocket. Dominic took it, claiming it was his by right. He thought of Isobel as his property, so naturally so was the chain."

I folded the confession carefully, my mind already racing ahead to what would come next. "Why are you giving me this?"

"Because Charlie was my son, too." The words came out in a rush, twenty years of suppressed truth finally finding its voice. "Not legally, not officially, but I helped raise him. I loved him. In my own way, I tried to shield him from the horrors of his past. But...I lacked the courage to do what I truly should have. And Dominic murdered him as surely as if he'd been a stranger on the street."

"This confession—if it's genuine—"

"It's genuine. I watched him write it through a crack in the door. But that's not all." Clara reached into her purse again, this time withdrawing a small object wrapped in tissue paper. "After he had gone to his office, I found this in his desk drawer, hidden behind a false back."

She unwrapped the tissue to reveal a diamond chain, its stones catching the late afternoon light that filtered through the boatshed's broken windows. But it wasn't the chain that made my breath catch—it was what was still attached to it. Dark stains that could only be blood, and caught in one of the links, a small piece of fabric that I felt sure matched the undershirt Charlie had been wearing when they pulled him from the harbour. This would be the final nail in Dominic's coffin.

"Poor Charlie," Clara said, continuing her narrative. "I was twenty-two years old and married to a man who could destroy me with a word. I had no choice but to go along with whatever he wanted of me." Clara's composure was beginning to crack. "But I tried to protect Charlie. I tried to be the mother he needed, even if I couldn't acknowledge him as my own stepson."

The harbour wind whistled through the gaps in the boatshed's walls, carrying with it the smell of salt and secrets that had finally found their way to the surface. I wrapped the chain carefully in my handkerchief, evidence that would hang a killer, no matter if his name was Dominic Latimer.

"What happens now?" Clara asked.

"Part of it is in play as we speak," I said. "The police are already gathering evidence of Dominic's other crimes, of all the sins of your family." I held up the wrapped chain. "The chain is now broken. The lies, the corruption, the whole rotten structure that your family built on other people's graves."

Clara nodded, and for the first time since I'd met her, she looked almost peaceful. "I've been carrying this weight for twenty years. It's time someone else carried it for a while."

We walked out of the boatshed together, leaving behind the shadows and the smell of decay. The city spread out before us, golden in the late afternoon light, beautiful and corrupt and full of the kind of secrets that destroyed families and built fortunes. Somewhere in its midst, Dominic Latimer was going about his business, thinking he'd covered his tracks well enough to escape justice.

He was wrong.

The chain was broken, and all the king's horses and all the king's men wouldn't be able to put it back together again. Justice might be blind, but she wasn't deaf, and she'd been listening at the door the night Charlie Bristow died.

It was time to make her heard.

~ Chapter 14 ~

The arrest happened at dawn, the way these things always did when the powerful were involved. No sirens, no crowds, no photographers from the *Herald* or the *Sun* to capture the moment when justice finally caught up with a man who thought his money could buy him immunity from the consequences of murder.

I stood in the shadows across the street from the Latimer mansion, watching as Tom Majors and two plainclothes detectives walked up the front steps with the quiet efficiency of men who'd done this before. The confession was in Tom's briefcase, along with the blood-stained chain and the forensic report that matched the fabric to Charlie's shirt and the blood to the boy's type. It was enough to hang a man, if the system worked the way it was supposed to. Tom had already obtained all the other evidence still situated in the Masonic Club's basement.

The door opened, and I caught a glimpse of Dominic Latimer in his dressing gown, his face pale in the morning light. There was a brief conversation, civilized and quiet, and then he was walking down the steps between the detectives like a man going to his club rather than his execution. No handcuffs, no rough handling—just the kind of courtesy that money could still buy, even at the end.

Tom caught my eye as they reached the police car and nodded almost imperceptibly. It was done. The chain that had bound the Latimer family together in lies and blood was, indeed, finally broken.

By noon, the story was already being shaped by the kind of men who specialized in turning ugly truths into palatable fiction. The newspapers would go on to report that Dominic Latimer had been arrested on charges of tax fraud and financial irregularities dating back to the war. The murder of Charlie Bristow would be handled quietly, through channels that the public would never see. There would be no trial, no sensational headlines, no detailed accounting of the corruption that had built a fortune on other people's graves.

"He'll plead guilty to manslaughter," Tom told me over drinks at the Criterion Hotel that evening. "Claims it was an accident, that he struck the boy in a moment of anger and panicked when he realized what he'd done. The prosecutors are happy to take it—saves them the trouble of a messy trial that might embarrass important people."

"And the rest of it? The profiteering, the political payoffs? All the evidence we gathered?"

"That's being handled by other departments. Quietly. The kind of justice that happens behind closed doors, where the only witnesses are accountants and tax collectors."

I took a drink of my beer and looked up toward the ceiling, thinking about the different kinds of justice that existed in a city like Sydney. There was the kind that happened in courtrooms, with judges and juries and newspaper reporters taking notes. And then there was the kind that happened in back rooms and government offices, where fortunes were dismantled piece by piece and powerful men simply disappeared from public view.

"What about the family?"

"Isobel left this morning. Train to Melbourne, then a steamer to Singapore. She won't be back." Tom's voice was matter-of-fact, but I could hear the regret underneath. "Clara's been committed to a private sanitarium. Nervous breakdown, the doctors say. She'll be well cared for."

I understood. The Latimer family was closing ranks, protecting its own even as it cut away the diseased parts. Isobel would live quietly somewhere in the Empire, supported by what remained of the family fortune. Clara would spend her remaining years in comfortable exile, her knowledge of the family's secrets safely contained behind sanitarium walls.

"And the chain?"

"Evidence locker, for now. Eventually it'll be returned to the estate, I suppose. Though I can't imagine anyone wanting to wear it after what happened."

The chain. I thought about the generations of women who'd worn it—several generations of young women who had died prematurely, each one carrying the weight of family secrets that had ultimately destroyed them all. It was a fitting symbol for the whole rotten structure, beautiful on the surface but tainted by the blood that had been spilled to acquire it.

"There's something else," Tom said, lowering his voice. "The yacht. The one where Charlie was killed."

"What about it?"

"It was sold yesterday. To a businessman from Perth. Cash sale, no questions asked. By the time the new owner takes possession, it'll have been completely refurbished. New paint, new fittings, new name. You'd never know what happened there."

Another piece of evidence disappearing into the bureaucratic maze that protected the powerful from the consequences of their actions. The yacht would sail under a new name, its bloody history erased as thoroughly as if it had never existed. The harbour would keep its secrets, as it always had.

We drank in silence for a while, watching the early evening crowd filter in and out of the hotel bar. Office workers and shop girls, dock workers and clerks, all of them going about their lives unaware that justice had been served in their city that day, quietly and without fanfare.

"Do you think it's enough?" I asked finally.

"Enough for what?"

"For Charlie. For justice."

I thought about the boy I'd seen in the photographs, the earnest face that had carried his mother's eyes and his father's stubborn pride. He'd died because he'd wanted something that should have been his by right—recognition, legitimacy, a place in the family that had created him and then discarded him like an unwanted reminder of past sins.

"No," Tom said. "It's not enough. But it's what we've got."

The sun was setting over Sydney Harbour, painting the water gold and red. Somewhere out there, in the depths where Charlie Bristow had been found, the harbour was keeping its other secrets—the ones that would never be recovered, never be judged, never be avenged. The city rolled on, indifferent to the small dramas of justice and revenge that played out in its shadows.

Tom finished his drink and stood to leave. "I'll be in touch if anything else comes up. Though I doubt it will."

"What happens to the case file?"

"The official one gets filed away. Closed case, solved to the satisfaction of all parties." He paused at the door. "But I'll keep a copy. Just in case."

I understood. In case the official version of events ever needed to be challenged, in case someone with more courage than sense decided to dig deeper into the Latimer family's past. It was a small act of defiance, but it was something.

After Tom left, I walked back to my office through the darkening streets. The city was transforming itself for the evening shift—the shop girls going home, the night workers coming out, the whole complex machinery of urban life shifting into its nocturnal rhythm. I thought about the chain of events that had brought me to this moment, the small decisions and chance encounters that had led from a woman in a grey coat to a killer in custody.

The office felt different when I got there, as if the resolution of the case had changed something fundamental about the space. The photographs were still spread across my desk, but they looked like artifacts from someone else's story now. I gathered them up and locked them away in my safe, along with the other secrets that people had paid me to keep.

I poured myself a whiskey and sat down at my desk, thinking about chains and justice and the way the past never really stayed buried, no matter how deep you tried to dig the grave. The Latimer case was closed, the family scattered to the winds like leaves in a harbour wind. Dominic would spend his remaining years in prison, Clara would live out her days in comfortable exile, and Isobel would disappear into the Empire, carrying her secrets with her. But Charlie and

Margaret would have to settle for a poor version of justice. I could only hope it would be enough for them.

The chain that had bound them together in lies and blood was finally broken. But I knew that somewhere in the city, other chains were being forged, other secrets were being buried, other families were building their fortunes on other people's graves. That was the way of things in a place like Sydney—corruption and wealth moving in cycles, like the tides that washed the harbour clean twice a day.

Outside my window, the city lights were beginning to twinkle like stars, beautiful and distant and full of secrets that would never be fully told. I finished my whiskey and put on my coat, ready to walk back out into the city that had shaped me and that I'd learned to navigate like a sailor reading the wind. I had things to work through in my mind before I headed home to my apartment.

The case was closed, but the work continued. There would be other clients, other mysteries, other chains to break. That was the nature of the business I'd chosen, and the nature of the city I'd made my home.

Justice had been served, quietly and without fanfare. It wasn't perfect, but it was what we had. Sometimes, that was enough. Because it had to be.

~ Epilogue ~

It was a few weeks after the arrest had taken place, and the case had already long vanished from the public consciousness like an unwanted house guest, but I was still ruminating over all that had happened. As I walked, the city blurred at the edges as dusk settled in, soft and damp, like a handkerchief pressed to a bleeding lip. Fog clung low to the ground, brushing the boots of passers-by and flattening the sound of footsteps into whispers. Gaslamps flickered along the edge of Hyde Park, their light stretched thin by the mist. I walked without direction, following the winding paths like they might lead somewhere I hadn't already been.

Somewhere behind me, a tram screeched to a halt, the bell sharp as a slap. A burst of voices spilled out, then faded into the hush. The fog was swallowing everything — buildings, streetlights, people. Even the war memorial, just visible through the trees, looked like something half-remembered from a dream.

Hyde Park had always felt like a place between things— between the courts and the churches, between the docks and the Domain, between where you'd been and where you thought you were going. That night, it felt like the city's conscience. Silent, fogbound, full of statues that couldn't look away.

I passed a man asleep on a bench, collar pulled up, hat over his eyes. A tram conductor on break, maybe. Or someone who'd once had somewhere to be. The kind of man you could pass a hundred times and never see. Sydney was full of them. Full of people who had made choices that never stopped echoing.

A pair of women walked past me, one laughing softly at something the other said. The sound faded behind them like ripples in a pond. It made me think of voices I hadn't heard in days. Or weeks. Hard to tell anymore.

The trees above me creaked in the breeze. I watched the branches move like tired arms reaching out for something just out of reach.

Then I heard it: the sharp slap of shoes on wet stone, the sudden lift of a child's laughter.

A boy in a school uniform tore past me, satchel swinging, cap askew, his arms out like wings as he dodged around the benches. For a moment, he was the only thing alive in the world — all motion and light and freedom. Then the fog took him, and he was gone.

I stood there for a long moment, watching as the child scampered away. You see a boy like that, running like there's nothing behind him, and you start to wonder. Not just where he's going, but whether he knows. Whether any of us do.

Whether it's the future we're running toward—or something darker we're trying to outrun.

The past doesn't vanish just because we close a door or cross a border. It follows, silent as fog, soft as memory. It lives in the pauses between words, in the faces of strangers, in the sound of a bell you haven't heard since childhood. Most of the time, we pretend it's not there. But it is. Waiting.

I let these thoughts and more flitter away and started walking again.

Behind me, the city breathed — trams rolling, horns echoing from the harbour, doors opening and closing. Sydney carried on, steady as ever. Blind to the broken things inside it. Or maybe just used to them.

Ahead, the path curved through the trees, vanishing into mist. I followed it without hurry. No appointments. No clients. Just a coat, a scar, and whatever came next.

You can't escape the past. Not really.

But sometimes, for a little while, in a quiet park at dusk— you can pretend you have.

~ Author's Note ~

This story really did come out of nowhere, but in a way, it had been percolating in my mind for some years. I've long been a fan of the works of Raymond Chandler and Ross MacDonald, both unparalleled masters of the noir detective genre. I've devoured all the stories of the former, and am currently tracking down all from the latter. While reading one of the MacDonald Lew Archer novels, a thought came to me...could I, perhaps, try to write just such a novel? This was a few years ago now, I think, and I busied myself creating the major characters and even some of the supporting characters of, what became, this book you are now currently holding in your hands.

But that was where it remained. I tried to start the actual writing process, but then my daughter was born, the pandemic came along and everything just fell by the wayside. Also, I was having some difficulty crafting a story with the same sort of complexity and nuance that a master like MacDonald did so easily, and so well. I didn't want to publish something that was a piece of rubbish, all the while acknowledging I could never equal, let alone beat, the likes of MacDonald or Chandler.

The years went by, and in more recent times, I've returned to my *Wraith* series of books with a vengeance, making up for lost time. I've also since read a lot of Lew Archer novels. I think I finally have a take on this genre now, and so I was finally able to crack this nut. It's a short book, it's my first such gumshoe book, but I think it turned out okay. At least I hope so. And I hope you agree with me.

As always, I'd like to thank my family for always supporting me, my various colleagues (you know who you are) and my loyal readers. I hope you stick with me with this new series of books I have planned. An Australian period detective series of books in the Chandler/MacDonald vein...that's just the sort of thing I'd like to read myself.

As I write this, I've outlined several further books in the George 'Magpie' Collins mystery series and written the first chapter of the next in the series, *The Black Seam* (a sneak peek is coming up). I'll get to those as my schedule allows. Perhaps one a year if I'm able. If you enjoyed this one (and I hope you did), then please keep an eye out for those further books in the series.

Frank Dirscherl aka Len Driscoll
Wollongong, 2025

THE BLACK SEAM
~ Sneak peek ~

Here is a special sneak peek at the following novel in the series, *The Black Seam*. Please enjoy chapter 1 of this exciting book...

~ Chapter 1 ~

The morning rain had left Castlereagh Street looking like a dark mirror, reflecting the grey October sky back at itself. I was nursing my second cup of black coffee and trying to make sense of the morning paper's headlines when she walked into my office. She didn't knock—just opened the door like she owned the place and stood there dripping rain onto my hardwood floor.

Dr. Eleanor Whitman, as I was soon to discover, was the sort of woman who'd learned to carry herself like she had answers to questions other people hadn't thought to ask yet. Tall, with steel-grey hair pulled back in a way that suggested she didn't have time for nonsense, she wore a dark wool coat that probably cost more than most blokes made in a month. But there was something in her eyes that didn't match the confident posture—a kind of hunted look that I'd seen before in people who'd found themselves in deeper water than they'd bargained for.

"Mr. Collins?" Her voice had the educated tones of someone who'd spent years telling other people what was wrong with them. "I need your help."

I gestured to the chair across from my desk. "That's what the sign on the door says. Though most people make an appointment first."

She sat down carefully, keeping her handbag clutched tight in her lap. "I couldn't risk using the telephone. This is...delicate."

I'd heard that word before. In my experience, when respectable people said something was delicate, it usually meant someone was about to get hurt. I leaned back in my chair and waited for her to tell me about it.

"My name is Dr. Eleanor Whitman. I run a private psychiatric clinic in Woollahra," she began, then stopped as if the words had got stuck somewhere between her brain and her mouth. "I specialise in treating patients with...difficult conditions. Depression, anxiety, trauma from the war."

"Worthwhile work," I said, though I kept my voice neutral. In my line of business, you learned not to judge people by their professions—sometimes the most respectable jobs hid the darkest secrets.

She opened her handbag and pulled out an envelope. The paper was expensive, cream-coloured, the sort that told you whoever wrote it had money to burn. "Three days ago, I received this."

I took the envelope and slid out a single sheet of paper. The message was typed, probably on a Remington by the look of the letters, and whoever had written it knew how to get to the point:

Dr. Whitman,

You have broken the seam of trust that should exist between doctor and patient. The methods you have used go beyond unorthodox—they are criminal. I have evidence of your violations of medical ethics and patient confidentiality that would destroy your career and see you struck off the medical register.

If you wish to avoid public exposure, you will place £500 in unmarked notes in a suitcase and leave it at the luggage counter at Central Station on Friday at 3 PM. Further instructions will follow.

Remember, doctor—broken seams will be exposed.

I read it through twice, then looked up at her. "Any idea who might have written this?"

"None." Her voice was steady, but I could see the tension in the way she held her shoulders. "I've been over my patient files, my staff, everyone who might have access to confidential information. I simply don't know."

"The note mentions breaking the seam of trust. Methods that go beyond unorthodox. Care to elaborate on what that might mean?"

She was quiet for a long moment, staring at her hands. When she looked up, there was something vulnerable in her expression that hadn't been there before. "I use some...experimental techniques in my practice. Hypnosis, combined with certain pharmaceutical aids. Nothing harmful, but perhaps not entirely conventional."

"Pharmaceutical aids?"

"Mild sedatives. Sodium pentothal in very small doses. It helps patients access suppressed memories, traumatic experiences they've buried." She leaned forward slightly. "Mr. Collins, I want you to understand—I would never deliberately harm a patient. Everything I do is in service of helping them heal."

I nodded and set the letter down on my desk. "Tell me about your patients. Anyone leave recently under difficult circumstances?"

"Several, actually." She hesitated. "It's not uncommon in psychiatric treatment. Patients often resist therapy when it becomes...challenging."

"Anyone in particular stand out?"

"There was a young man. Robert Ashford. He was the son of Charles Ashford, the mining magnate. Robert had been through a traumatic experience—an accident at one of his father's mines where several workers were killed. He felt responsible, developed severe depression and anxiety."

"When did he leave your care?"

"Two months ago. He...he took his own life shortly after."

I felt that familiar tightness in my chest that came when a case started to show its teeth. "Suicide?"

"The coroner ruled it accidental death. Robert had been drinking, fell from a cliff in the Blue Mountains where he was staying." She looked down at her hands again. "But I knew Robert. He was getting better, or so I thought. The suicide...it shocked me."

"And you think there might be a connection between his death and this blackmail?"

"I don't know. Maybe. Robert had been making remarkable progress, and then suddenly he left treatment and was dead within a fortnight." She met my eyes. "Mr. Collins, I need you to find out who's doing this to me. I can't pay that money—I don't have it, for one thing. But more importantly, I won't be extorted by someone who doesn't understand the complexities of psychiatric treatment."

I studied her face, trying to read the truth behind the professional mask. In my experience, people who claimed they were being blackmailed usually had something worth blackmailing them about. But there was something in her manner that suggested she was more frightened than guilty.

"My fee is five pounds a day plus expenses," I said finally. "And I'll need complete access to your clinic, your staff, and your records."

"Of course." She reached into her handbag and pulled out a roll of notes. "Here's twenty pounds as a retainer. Will that be sufficient?"

I took the money and locked it in my desk drawer. "Tell me about your staff. Anyone who might have access to confidential patient information?"

"There's Patricia Mills, my nurse. She's been with me for eight months. And James Hartwell, who handles the administrative side—appointments, billing, that sort of thing. He's been with me for two years."

"Anyone else?"

"A cleaning woman who comes in twice a week. Mrs. Davies. She's been with me since I opened the clinic three years ago."

I made notes as she talked, already forming a mental picture of the people I'd need to interview. "One more question, Doctor. This experimental treatment you mentioned—hypnosis and pharmaceutical aids. Ever have any patients react badly to it?"

She was quiet for a long moment. "Psychiatric treatment is always risky, Mr. Collins. The human mind is fragile, and sometimes trying to heal it can cause... complications."

"What kind of complications?"

"Memory issues. Confusion. In rare cases, patients might develop false memories or become unable to distinguish between real and imagined experiences." She stood up, smoothing down her coat. "But I want to emphasise—I would never deliberately harm a patient. Everything I do is guided by my oath to do no harm."

I walked her to the door, noting how she moved with the careful precision of someone who'd learned to control every gesture. "I'll start with your clinic tomorrow morning. In the meantime, don't do anything about this demand. If whoever wrote this is watching, we want them to think you're going to cooperate."

She nodded and shook my hand. Her grip was firm, but I could feel the slight tremor in her fingers. "Thank you, Mr. Collins. I hope you can resolve this quickly."

After she left, I sat back down at my desk and read the blackmail note again. The phrase 'broken seams will be exposed' stuck in my mind. It had the ring of someone who thought they were being clever, but it might also be a clue. In my experience, blackmailers usually couldn't resist showing off how much they knew.

I pulled out a fresh notebook and wrote "Dr. Eleanor Whitman" at the top of the first page. Underneath, I made a list: Patricia Mills, James Hartwell, Mrs. Davies, Robert Ashford (deceased). Then I added a question mark and the word 'others.'

The rain had stopped, and pale sunlight was filtering through the grimy windows of my office. I could hear the traffic on Castlereagh Street picking up as the lunch crowd began to move. My stomach reminded me that I'd skipped breakfast, but I wanted to think through what I'd learned before I headed over to the Masonic Club for a meal.

Dr. Whitman's story had the feel of truth to it, but there were gaps—things she hadn't told me or didn't want to tell me. The experimental treatments, the connection to Robert Ashford's death, the specific phrasing of the blackmail note. Someone knew enough about her practice to cause real damage, and they were professional enough to typewrite their demands rather than hand-write them.

I locked the blackmail note in my desk drawer next to the retainer money and grabbed my coat. The case felt like it had depths I hadn't seen yet, but that was nothing new. In my line of work, the surface was usually the least interesting part of any story.

As I walked over to the club next door, I found myself thinking about seams and broken links. Seams, like chains, were only as strong as their weakest point. The trick was finding that weakness and applying just enough pressure to make the whole thing fall apart.

Someone was applying pressure to Dr. Eleanor Whitman. The question was whether they were trying to break her, or whether she was just one link in something much larger.

~ Also Available ~

VALLEY OF EVIL

The Wraith Dread Avenger of the Underworld #2
VALLEY OF EVIL
Frank Dirscherl

After the horror the Cobra unleashed upon Metro City, Paul Sanderson has recuperated, regained his strength and focus, and the city has been rebuilt while its citizens have slowly started to regroup and move forward. Into this relative calm marches Ma Tzi, the Hong Kong drug lord, who senses a weakness in resident crime lord Robert Latham's hold on the city and intends to exploit that in any way necessary. And at any cost.

NOW AVAILABLE!

www.glowingeyesmedia.com

The Wraith Dread Avenger of the Underworld #4
CULT OF THE DAMNED
Frank Dirscherl

With the city back firmly in his grasp, crime lord and entrepreneur Robert Latham is celebrating by bankrolling Metro City's 200th anniversary gala year, which includes the unveiling of a never-before-seen ancient Aztec stone carving—the Cortes Stone—at the City Gallery, a carving that has thrilled the scientific and artistic communities, but infuriated the monstrous Aztekoth.

NOW AVAILABLE!

www.glowingeyesmedia.com

CRY OF THE WEREWOLF

The Wraith Dread Avenger of the Underworld #5

CRY OF THE WEREWOLF

Frank Dirscherl

Having gone through ordeal after ordeal, Paul Sanderson (aka The Wraith Dread Avenger of the Underworld ®) and his love Leena Patterson, decide to take a long overdue vacation. However, their idyll is soon shattered by an attack by a creature nobody thought could possibly exist—a werewolf. Soon, an evil so heinous makes himself known, and only The Wraith could possibly defeat it.

NOW AVAILABLE!

www.glowingeyesmedia.com

The Wraith Dread Avenger of the Underworld #6

SWAMP WITCH OF SATAN'S FOREST

Frank Dirscherl & Ray MacKay

On their way home from their mountain vacation which was anything but, Paul Sanderson (aka The Wraith) and his love Leena Patterson are waylaid by a mysterious cry for help, and are unwittingly drawn into the forest—and the web—of the alluring Swamp Witch.

NOW AVAILABLE!

www.glowingeyesmedia.com

The Wraith Dread Avenger of the Underworld #7
VENDETTA
Frank Dirscherl

After having been betrayed by crime lord, Robert Latham, and defeated by The Wraith, Crossfire has returned to cause mayhem and carnage at every turn. His ultimate aim? The utter destruction of all his enemies, and he doesn't care who gets in his way.

NOW AVAILABLE!

www.glowingeyesmedia.com

Books of Judgment Book Two
SERPENT RISING
Frank Dirscherl & Greg Gick

The never-before-told origin story of The Wraith's arch nemesis the Cobra. Who he is, how he came to be, and how his and the original Paul Sanderson's life intertwined at key moments to cause them to become deadly adversaries. It's all here!

NOW AVAILABLE!

Books of Judgment Book Three

RISING SON

Frank Dirscherl & Adam Oravec

Robert Latham, Metro City's pre-eminent businessman and entrepreneur. He's also the head of the largest crime cartel on the east coast, the web in the center of the city's web of evil. But how did he become the all-powerful figure within the city. Growing up with nothing, he built his empire from the ground up, through strength, determination, and cold-blooded intimidation.

COMING SOON!

www.glowingeyesmedia.com

About the Type

Garamond is a group of many old-style serif typefaces, originally those designed by Parisian craftsman Claude Garamond and other 16th century French engravers, and now many modern revivals. Though his name was written as 'Garamont' in his lifetime, the typefaces are generally spelled 'Garamond'. **Garamond Normal,** used in this book, is one of those modern revivals.

Join FRANK DIRSCHERL and LEN DRISCOLL with Glowing Eyes Media on social media!

facebook.com/glowingeyesmedia

@glowingeyesmedia

instagram.com/glowingeyesmedia

@glowingeyesmedia.bsky.social

glowingeyesmedia.proboards.com

All Glowing Eyes Media, The Wraith, George 'Magpie' Collins novels, comics and merchandise can be obtained directly from the Glowing Eyes Media website –
www.glowingeyesmedia.com

www.ingramcontent.com/pod-product-compliance
Lightning Source LLC
Chambersburg PA
CBHW070757280626
47162CB00016B/1416